GINNY

GINNY

MORTON COOPER

CUTTING EDGE

ISBN-13: 978-1-962896-42-9

Published by
Cutting Edge Books
PO Box 8212
Calabasas, CA 91372
www.cuttingedgebooks.com

CHAPTER ONE

IT BEGAN WHEN HIS WIFE went out of town for the summer.

It would have happened anyway, of course, even if Fran had stayed in New York with him through those hot, frenzied days when Jim Creighton's career began to boom. Unless you were insane or dull witted or an emotional eunuch, you didn't back away when someone as vitally available as Ginny Grant appeared.

Sure, he knew, it would have happened anyway—the lies, the deceptions, even the tragic violence. The fact that Fran drove up to Cabott Island with the Fraziers on the Thursday evening before the Fourth of July weekend, to escape the heavy holiday traffic, simply helped to speed its beginning.

They had been living in that far too elegant apartment just a building away from Sutton Place for a month when Ira and Madge Frazier invited Fran and Jim to spend as much of the summer as they chose with them at their house on Cabott. "The missus and I specialize in fresh air and open pores up there in God's country, Jim boy," Ira had announced one night when the four had been together. "Good old fashioned community sings when we get in the mood, and a couple days fishing that'll make you feel like that steel drivin' man. Whatzisname."

Fran, understandably, had liked the idea; she hated New York in the summer, and certainly his crazy work schedules over the past five months, of darting from the radio mike to the TV cameras, weren't designed to make her the most contented of wives.

Jim, on the other hand, had no intention of being included in the plan. Not only would this be his most hectic summer in town, but he found Ira Frazier to be an almost monumental bore. Ira was an active third of Kermit, Frazier and Hoyt, one of the most outrageously successful ad agencies in the city, and indirectly his firm was paying the freight for a few of Jim's shows. But after fifteen or twenty minutes of listening to his Visiting Martians stories and his ridiculously-stamped Madison-Avenue lingo, Jim was usually ready to slug him.

"I'll get up there as often as I can," he lied to Fran on that Thursday, the same day Evelyn Shoreham, his and Bucky Stander's chief researcher, had brought Ginny Grant to his office for the first introduction. "Except for part of Saturdays, though, I can't step out of the station for a minute, you know. Not till September, when I can get these newscasts off my neck."

"Maybe this Saturday," Fran said hopefully. "The day after tomorrow. You can sleep over Saturday night and come in on Sunday for the *Butcher, Baker* show. That's just a guest-panel thing. You don't have to rehearse for that."

"You forget. I have the news show at six on Saturday."

"But six ..." she persisted gently, never pushing him because Fran wouldn't have known how to push. "If you come up Saturday morning, you'd have the whole morning, and then you could ..."

"Fran, you know that won't work. It takes close to three hours to get up to that Godforsaken place and another three to get back. What would I have time for? One of Big Ira's stories about how John D. Rockefeller once gave him a shiny new dime? You're the one who can use the vacation, anyway. These past five months have been one adjustment after another for you."

"Well ..." she began uncertainly and then let it drop. He made a run for it before the Fraziers showed up, after making a few sketchy promises about keeping in touch with her.

❧ ❧ ❧

The next morning, the morning it began, he came awake at five, thinking of Ginny Grant, thinking that it would be only a matter of time before he made the right pass at her.

Exhaustedly, his eyes aching, his body yearning for more sleep, he switched on the night-table light and tuned in the 5 A.M. news. It was a routine he'd been performing for the past two and a half years, since he'd landed his own eight o'clock radio news show on WRBS. Chet Mitchell's broadcast told him pretty much what he'd find in store when he arrived at the studio at a quarter of seven—whether any crisis had developed since the night before, whether he could expect more than the normal amount of pre-show preparation.

He lighted his first cigarette as he looked around at the still foreign bedroom of the still foreign apartment which half a year ago he could not have dreamed of having. He tried to focus his attention to Chet's report and discovered that the Grant girl's exquisite perfume scent was returning again.

The routine of a news broadcast at eight in the morning, at noon, and at six in the evening would continue until Labor Day, when the local contracts would be up and his interview show on television would go network. Only two more months of this rugged grind to go, he attempted to console himself as he zigzagged the cigarette into the tray. If he could hold off without going nuts until then, the pressures were guaranteed to lessen a little. Or so Bucky Stander, his producer and partner, kept assuring him. *I am smack in the middle of a souped-up treadmill during this rainy Fourth of July season*, he thought. *I am restless and nervous and worried because I'd never asked for this kind of action, never wanted this fantastically fancy apartment or to have waiters at Twenty-One and Harwyn salivate when they saw me coming. And*

I still need Bucky to supply the answers for me. The abrupt switch from a bourbon and water at Costello's on 3rd Avenue to a bourbon and water at El Morocco is still a weird jolt, and I'm conscious at odd moments of the day that my teeth are clenched and my palms are a little clammy.

But now, at 5:15 as the incessant rain lashed against the picture windows, he swung his legs over the side of the twin bed and found he could look forward to the back breaking day with increasing excitement.

He would see her at the office. If she looked at him again in that pervasive, knowing, suavely-receptive way she'd looked at him the day before, the whole daffy meaning of having turned into a comet without being ready for it would begin to be bearable.

Although the necessary lights were on in the dinette after he shaved, showered and dressed, it was still a gloomy, depressing morning that promised no letup of rain. The Fraziers had been smart to take off for the island a day earlier than they'd planned. Mrs. Wentsmann, the ancient German housekeeper-cook whom Bucky had recommended he hire ("What do you mean 'extravagance'?" Bucky had barked. "What're you going to do, have the newspapers say your wife still scrubs the kitchen floor?"), had his eggs and sausages ready for him.

"Herr Creighton," she nodded brusquely. "Goot morning."

"Good morning," he nodded, sitting at his place and glumly regarding the seed which floated in his orange juice. He indicated that he wished to bury himself in the morning *Times*.

"Iss raining."

"Yes."

"Der Frau Creighton. Ve hope she got better der veather up there than ve got down here."

"Yes, I hope so." He wondered again, as he chewed at the eggs which by some miraculous inspiration she had learned to turn into shoe leather, why Mrs. Wentsmann needed to be here on a twenty-four-hour-a-day basis. What was Bucky paying her, in Jim's money, for her nebulous services? Certainly with Fran away he'd be having even fewer meals at home. The obvious answer—only for show; you hired unnecessary help so that it would look good—made him wince. But then renting an eight-room apartment at $675 a month, four rooms of which neither he nor Fran ever bothered to set foot in, was silly, too, and he'd allowed Bucky and a few butterflies of vice-presidents at RBS to talk him into taking it.

From the dinette he could look out onto the living room, which clearly was more than half the size of Rhode Island. Fran and that rather fruity interior decorator from Lexington Avenue had worked on it and put it together in quiet, good taste, and yet the overall effect was a garish one. Vulgar in its very bigness (there were no children, there never could be any children), loud in its snobbish proclamations of sudden wealth, and garish as hell.

For an oppressive moment, after Mrs. Wentsmann skittered back to the kitchen, he observed the bowling alley of a living room with a fleetingly honest perspective, and the jitters commenced again. What did they need it all for? What did they need with a Mrs. Wentsmann, who had a talent for infuriating him? What were they doing with a home that was about as cozy as Yankee Stadium, just because someone had suggested a few months ago that it would be fitting for Jim Creighton, the new white-haired boy of TV?

"You vill eat here sopper tonight?" Mrs. Wentsmann inquired, coming back and hovering. "I fix sopper?"

"Ah—I'm not sure yet," he said. He'd have to remember to tell her to cut it out. But, he thought irritably, cut *what* out? How could he tell her she gave him the creeps just by looking at him? "I'll call you later and let you know."

"Please you will call early," she declared imperiously. "Iss different when der Frau Creighton iss here. Iss hard to plan sopper if you call der last minute."

Gradually he became aware of the imperiousness, of the dumb way he had let her take over. Fran tended to get ruffled and to pamper the dictatorial bitch when she got high-handed this way, but he was damned if she was going to get away with calling the shots. She'd come here a little under three weeks ago, complete with a heavy Master-Race manner that inferred he and Fran should raise their hands before leaving the room.

Folding his paper, he looked up at her, at the crisp spotlessness of her. "Suppose I get tied up and won't know *my* plans until late?" he baited, certain now that it was time for a showdown.

"Den you please vill eat in maybe restaurant," she advised, scooping up some invisible crumbs from the tablecloth. "I tell Mrs. Creighton vhen first I come here, sopper must be plan very early in day. I vork twenty-two year for Groeter family on Park Avenue, and alvays I know early in day."

The unquestioning mandate enraged him, but he forced himself to stay calm. "Let's get something straight, Mrs. Wentsmann," he said. "I pay you a salary every week, and if I remember right it's a good salary. You're going to tell *me* to eat in a restaurant?"

She was still unperturbed. "Iss only right," she nearly shrugged. "For twenty-two year I tell this to Herr Groeter and he iss happy." She was holding her ground but gradually her keen little eyes narrowed into a glare, as if she were daring him to upset her disciplined day.

Jim rose from the table, deciding to hell with the coffee. "Then it might be a fine idea if you just go back to Herr Groeter. And just as soon as you can pack your suitcase."

"*Voss iss?*"

"You heard *voss iss*. As long as I pay for the food in this apartment, no one—certainly not you—is going to tell me when to eat it. You know Mr. Stander, the man who sends you your salary every week. You'll find him at RBS this afternoon. I'll direct him to have your check ready for you, with two weeks extra pay or whatever it is you're supposed to get."

She stared at him, open mouthed, still not fully understanding, as he walked to get his briefcase and raincoat in the hall closet. "You iss dismissing me?"

"That's the idea. Leave the key with the head super in the basement."

Now that the fact began to dawn on her, she became rattled. "Never I am dismissed in mine whole life!"

"So you're having a new experience," he answered and walked out.

Well, it's starting, you great big success story, you, he thought grimly as he pressed the elevator button in the private vestibule. *No need to iron out a problem with a housekeeper, because you can always buy yourself a new one. You're on your way to becoming King of the Mountain and you can tell the help and the copy boys to snap to if you find yourself a trifle more tense than usual. In another few months you're going to be the titan of television and with it will come all the money in the world. And if you want to, you'll be able to tell the President of RBS to go take a flying leap. After that you can eat babies and bomb the Capitol for an encore.*

It was a hell of a way to begin the day. The day that would start the most desperate chain of events in his life.

John, the elevator operator who had just come on duty, helped to shift the mood a little.

"Morning, Mr, Creighton," he greeted. "Hey, you know I'm gonna sue you for keepin' me up so late at night, watchin' your program?" He opened with that line, in one form or another, every morning; it was getting tiresome but it was far from unpleasant.

"Thanks, John," he smiled. "Last night's wasn't one of the best, though."

"You kiddin'? That strip teaser sure came up with some snappy answers! Uh, say, my wife Kate, she made me promise to ask you a question. That stripteaser acted a little—well, funny every once in a while. Was she kind'a—well, drunk?"

"No," Jim lied in his teeth. "She was sober."

"Oh. Well, Kate, she wanted to know. You know women." He guffawed and winked. "Here's the lobby. Guess I'll have to sue you again tonight, huh?"

"Sue away, John. And thanks for the kind words. I appreciate them," he said, meaning it.

Except for an occasional swim with his kid brother Harry at the Bromley Gym, this early morning walk ritual to the studio was the only exercise he had the time or energy for and, come hangover or bad weather, he never neglected it. It was, for the most part, nearly the only time of the crowded day in which he could be alone and sift through the ribbons of ideas he was expected to keep coming up with. When Fran was in town, she usually raised the restrained roof a little if it was raining, as it definitely was now. But Fran never bore down with demands.

By the time he approached 56th and 3rd (it was ten minutes past six; he was running reasonably well ahead of time) he realized that the daydreaming about the Grant girl had come back again. He'd have to organize some comments about

De Gaulle's statement that the crisis in Algeria was becoming grave—both Chet Mitchell and *The Times* had given it a big play this morning—and he hadn't done any thinking at all about it yet.

The rain remained at a steady harshness as the scent of her remarkable perfume jammed his nostrils. Evelyn Shoreham, who prided herself on being the most accomplished news-desk researcher with a bosom in New York City, made an almost ostentatious point of hiring girl researchers for *Jim Creighton's Hot Spot* not because they had talent but because they were a mite less attractive than she. But her right hand gal, Helene Masters, who'd been so good at digging up the sob stuff, had quit to get married and a fill-in had been needed in a hurry. Virginia Grant, small but beautifully formed, with skin as clear and pale as liquid gold, had popped up. Because Jim and Bucky had been yelling for quick help, good looks or no good looks, Evelyn had brought her in.

He had spent no more than a minute with her the afternoon before. She had been self-assured, perhaps even unaware of him as anything other than an employer. For all he knew, she was married to a nice insurance salesman from Larchmont and she owned a raft of babies to whom she sped each night after work *(had Evelyn introduced her as Miss or Mrs.? why hadn't he made reserved attempt to find out?)*

He was making with the kid stuff, he knew, the small town infatuation stuff, and all of it was nuts for a greying old codger of thirty-six. Yet something subtly intangible about their hurried meeting—maybe a swift cocking of the eyebrow, maybe an innocent smile that had accidentally come across as something less than innocent—had made him want her. It had made him encourage Fran to join the Fraziers on their trip to Cabott Island. It had made him need to be—what? A wallthumping lover? A sexual athlete? A busy guy on the fast prowl? A man with a girl who could help him shake *off* the loneliness and fear?

Something.

Something he hadn't been for far too many years.

The regret, long before all of it would end, long before the tragedy was to come, would be overwhelming.

But there was no way of knowing that now, as he quickened his steps, wondering if she would come to work early.

He said the name aloud:

"Ginny."

CHAPTER TWO

M RS. WENTSMANN WAS THOROUGLY forgotten by the time he
reached the lobby of the Rockland Broadcasting System.
Anthony, the network's night elevator man who had barely recognized him during his first eight years here in the news department and his next two years as a spot news broadcaster, now
came awake with his phony geniality.

"What's it, raining out?" he kidded, grinning at the soaked
overcoat as Jim stepped in. "You look like you swum to work."

"Just about."

The cage hummed dully as it ascended the floors. "I got an
innersting compliment for you, Jimmy, gonna make your day
bright," Anthony enthused, turning around. He had two side
teeth missing. He had the same two teeth missing when Jim had
first come to work at RBS. "I carried Fat Red down in my box yesterday and he was talkin' about you to one of them creepy V.P.'s."

Fat Red was the private nickname for Flanders Bryce
Redmond, the absolute monarch of RBS. "So give," Jim said.

"Well, the V.P. starts jawin' about you, says he heard you give
this long speech last night at your six o'clock show about, what is
it, Alger or Aljiss or whatever ..."

"Algeria."

"That's what I say, and he asts if you was there in the War
or somep'm, you talk like you know so much about the joint.
And Fat Red takes this big. He says no, he missed the broadcast, but that Creighton, he's gonna be the biggest thing in TV

by Christmas, Fat Red says." Anthony beamed. "Well, is that a statement or is that a statement from Big Chief Stoneface?"

"That's plenty statement," Jim nodded, willing to let Anthony know he was moved. "Thanks for telling me. It doesn't exactly make me want to resign."

"From any of these here other lettuceheads, you can say what the hell. But Fat Red! Danny Darrow just signed up for his tenth straight year with RBS, I read yesterday in Wilson's column, and Fat Red still thinks Danny's a flash in the pan! That sort'a makes you like the head o' the damn world around here, don't it?"

"At least," Jim smiled and nodded again. Anthony had Redmond pegged exactly right. Some bright wags had tabbed Flanders Bryce Redmond the greatest mind of the Eighth Century. He was not a cruel or evil man, or even a man overly flecked with guile, but he did distinctly own artery-hardened ideas about what constituted the science of mass communication. Although he got a photograph of his imposing features in *Fortune* every so often, and was the recipient of countless plaques as The Father of Commercial Radio and Television, no one who worked under him, in any capacity, ever wholly understood how he had, very likely singlehandedly, turned Rockland Broadcasting into one of the most successful networks in the country, and in fewer than twenty years. Though he posed as a benevolent autocrat, Redmond's personal cultural tastes ran to dog acts and outsized bird calls. The walls of his mammoth office were plastered with straightfaced homily signs, such as "Grass Doesn't Grow on a Busy Street," "He Who Hesitates Is Lost," ... "Think." The bulk of his acquired knowledge was derived from the morning tabloids, and he regarded *Among My Souvenirs* as the quintessence of musical art. "Fat Red's concept of a perfect television evening," Clif Rawnsley of the news desk's foreign affairs department had once cracked, "would be composed of Lawrence Welk defying technology by offering square records, Liberace getting moist about his mother, and Rin Tin barking *Trees.*"

The cage door whined open at the 31st floor and Jim stepped out. "Thanks again, Anthony," he said. "I appreciate it. Honest."

"Forget it. Just keep Dominic in mind," Anthony called and came close to waving goodbye. Dominic, an old half-serious joke started five months before when *Jim Creighton's Hot Spot* had begun on the local New York outlet, was Anthony's favorite brother-in-law. Dominic ran a fourteen-inch bar and grille on Broadway in Washington Heights and was feverish for a publicity mention. Jim had found himself lulled into promising, over a period of time, that he would find a way to announce that Dominic sold the best hooch in the city, cheap.

"Any day now," he said.

Then he hurried to The Tank where Herb Graham, RBS' drunken politics expert and Clif Rawnsley were waiting to help him plan an attack on the De Gaulle-Algeria crisis. He told them he'd be with them in a minute, raced to his own quarters where he took a quickie shower and changed clothes, and hustled back to the meeting. Peg Robbins, the toothy secretary whose knee Clif liked to rub for good luck, had arrived to take what amounted to supersonic dictation from the three.

"What do you say, sport?" Clif called. "General De Gaulle ain't going to wait. Are you going to listen to my brilliant observations on Algeria, or do I have to ravish Peg for the seventeenth time? She couldn't be gladder, but I'm approaching my more senior years."

"Oh, you're just terrible!" Peg Robbins giggled, surreptitiously exhibiting a little more knee. Herb Graham, who would be able to turn in for the day in another half hour, merely grunted.

"So let's have vital discussion about world affairs, gentlemen," Jim said, taking his place at the table. "What's De Gaulle's first name again, Willie or Moe? I keep forgetting."

Because De Gaulle's ascension to the French military throne and his attitudes about the maintainance of that throne were of prime importance on this Fourth of July morning, the three dissected him from every conceivably intellectual and emotional angle, they thrust him into the hopper of the wire services' factual reports, and with Peg Robbin's help came up in forty-five minutes with what Jim knew would be a good 8 A.M. newscast. With blanching, the nub of it could be used on the noon show, slightly warmed over, and on the dinner show, too. He was grateful to Herb and Clif, who had attuned themselves to him so completely, even before that woolly afternoon in February when Fat Red had called him aside and told him his and Bucky's idea for an interview show on television just might go. It was a three-way friendship, a Toots Shor-Costello's-Absinthe House-Embers friendship which had meaning and solidity for him.

"You're making with the sparkle, sport," Clif advised him a few minutes before air time, "The minute you can cut me in on the fun, let me know. I couldn't be more suited to the free."

"Which means what?"

"Which means the Grant twist. I saw her give the first slither here yesterday under Aunt Evelyn's auspices. I dug her, man. But you—you flipped from here to Peking. All I can wish you in my aged state is good luck and Godspeed."

"Did it show that much, Clif?"

"Oh, drop the field of com, Pappy! You glommed her like you were ready for lunch at The Bronx Zoo. That whole thirty-second bit yesterday was the closest charade to *Romeo and Juliet* I've ever seen in my four days as Fat Red's footman. You're in like Errol, man!"

"And you're a thinking historian with high honors from Yale," Jim nagged, "but I don't entirely dig your beat. What language do you talk? Do you mean I might have a little luck with her?"

"Luck?" Clif crowed. "Pappy, you may have nothing more than a set of tonsils, the way Lobeck says,"—Steve Lobeck was *The Dispatch's* television critic who had been digging at Jim for months in his reasonably-powerful column—"but if you don't have it made by tonight at midnight, I'll eat all of last week's scripts! Without ketchup, yet!"

The quarter-hour show went well. At precisely thirty seconds before 8:15, Juggy, the engineer, made a circle with his thumb and forefinger and nodded through the huge pane of glass from the fishbowl. Jim gathered up the papers, buttoned his shirt collar, ran his fingers through his close-cropped, prematurely iron-grey hair *(Better take Bucky's advice and find time for a haircut)*, and went to the corridor to ride the elevator back up to his office.

"Goin' up," called Anthony as the cage door opened. The elevator was crowded as he stepped in. He smelled the perfume before he saw her. He turned, trusting he wouldn't look too obvious, and saw her fairly pinned to the rear wall behind a welter of freshly-starched people on their way to work.

She was looking at him and smiling.

Jim smiled and pantomined that a visit together on the way up was apparently impossible. With purposeful casualness he turned to the front again. *Let me play this right*, he thought as he rolled up the morning's manuscript and tapped it against his palm. *Let me start it so that it promises to look like something. No pouncing. No indication that there's going to be chasing around desks. If it doesn't go right, from the start, it will fold like a dollar-bridge table. Just let me act as if I know what I'm doing....*

The door opened again on the 31st floor and he was the first one out. He stood aside as six or seven people emerged. The time seemed interminably long before she came out, still smiling yesterday's piquant, intimate smile. Or were piquant and intimate the right words to describe her full and yet elusive smile? The word 'intimate' summoned up the rather gross, French postcard image of pleasures that had gone before or pleasures to boldly come. And the smile neoned no such thing. There was too thoroughly a well-scrubbed look about her, a joyous-tennis-player look, a Rheingold-Girl look without quite the vapid eyes and ostentatious pronouncements of virginity, a ginger-ale look with just the faintest shot of whiskey.

No. Last night's and this morning's fantasies about her being the owner and operator of dark, wild passions weren't immediately evident now.

"Hi," she greeted. "Maybe it's true we'll all be destroyed by the H-Bomb. But before that we'll be destroyed by crowded elevators."

"Do what I do," he said, starting to walk beside her down the narrow corridor. "Sell breakfast cereal on the radio. That way, you get into the elevator last and you get off first."

"Good idea," she nodded. "Why didn't I think of that sooner?" He would have to learn, probably from Evelyn, what she was doing at a $65 a week job like this, a creatively-thankless job at best, when she could be making more money from selling hardware or kiddies' toys. She was young—certainly she was no more than twenty-five—but a researcher accepted jobs at $65 a week these days only if she were nineteen years old and breaking into the nutty business, or if she were seventy-five years old and waving goodbye to all the ships that were sailing away.

He made a furtive mental note that she wore no rings on her fingers.

Bucky Stander materialized suddenly from nowhere, it seemed, and touched Jim's shoulder. "Jim, see you a minute," he croaked and then waddled industriously into his office.

"Uh … see you," he said to her and watched her nod briskly. She kept on, a marvelously-joined girl with dark, deep blue eyes that carried only a vague suggestion that she was more than willing to be amused. He kept watching until she disappeared into Evelyn's office down the corridor. She paused for an instant, just before she entered it, to glance back at him.

"How'd the eight o'clocker go, Jim? I got tied up and I missed it," Bucky rumbled in a restless, who-cares voice. Leonard Lyons of *The Post* had tabbed the two of them The Mutt and Jeff of RBS. While Jim was six-four and lanky, Bucky barely topped five-four and, despite the Brooks-Brothers suits and impeccable barbering, was unpleasantly obese. His voice was reminiscent of the cranking of rusty motors and some of the more sensitive souls around the department found him overbearing and too eager to dominate all the proceedings. He was, however, a hell of a smart producer and even the tangerines who wanted to give him the shiv acknowledged that he knew exactly what he was doing all the time.

"Not bad." Jim sat as Bucky waved a beefy hand in the direction of the couch. "Usually on holidays we have to go scrounging for news, but this morning I had to actually cut. Algeria and Alaska and that triple murder in Columbus Circle …"

"Yeah," Bucky replied in that tone that inferred he was never quite listening. "Speaking of Alaska, I got hold of that schoolmarm from Fairbanks last night. The one who's been yakking for statehood to presidents for the past two hundred and twelve administrations. I mentioned her to you, didn't I? Names's Schofield?"

"That's right."

"If she's not too loony-sounding, if she can make a little sense without the gush, we'll slip her into your six o'clock show tonight for say a five-minute interview about what she thinks the new statehood will mean. Evelyn's having breakfast with her at The Hampshire House in about a half hour from now. She'll feel her out and report in a yes or no by ten. If it's 'yes', we'll write up about six or eight loaded questions. Ought to be a cinch. All you have to——"

"Well, wait a moment, Bucky," Jim interrupted, never quite sure how free he could be with him. "I think an editorial on the French crisis should take precedence. I've been doing a little work on it. I was planning to phone Fletch Gavin to come in. He just flew in from there last week and ..."

"Crap," Bucky dismissed and reached for a cigar from the fancy gold humidor, the one his wife Jeanne had brought him from Rome. "Let me size 'em up when news is timely, will you, Jimmy? Alaska right now is red headline sensation stuff and everyone'll eat it up. Who's going to follow a military chant from Gavin, some dirty-nailed egghead from Kew Gardens? Leave that intellectual bit to Murrow."

"But it's important ..."

"Important, hell. What the meatballs can identify themselves with right off the top is what's important. You collar any solid citizen at the corner of 44th Street and ask him to locate Algiers, and you know what he'll answer? It's a movie from twenty years ago with Charles Boyer and Hedy La Marr, the one where he takes her to the Casbah; they all saw it on the Late Show. Never give 'em more than they're going to take, Jimmy, if you want to sell your soapsuds and suppositories. The lousiest blunder anyone in this racket can make is to accuse the meatheads of wanting to learn something past how to make a dame say 'yes' faster and better."

Moving in the chair uncomfortably, Jim lighted a cigarette. "You know something, Bucky? You're more and more starting to sound like Fat Red, Marie Antoinette's psychiatrist."

"Oh, beat it with that holier than us junk! Your darling solid citizens want to be informed about the intricacies of mankind about as much as turtles want to go the eighty-yard run. You remember May of this fiscal year, pal? Was the world any more on the brink of going to pieces than it was this May? Khrushchev and Dulles and Nasser and Mao and the recession were talking up a storm, and everybody was ready to go to hell in a bucket. And then what happened to part the waves? Vivian Barclay died. Vivian Barclay, beloved star of stage, screen and bent spoon suddenly took an overdose of H and kicked off. And for five solid days were radio, television, newspapers and over-the-fence gossip full of anything else? Tell me, O Noble Thirster After Truth, did anything else really matter a straw in this whole grand land for five full days?"

Jim's determination to argue—the arguments with the meticulously calculating Bucky made him feel in the company of Clarence Darrow when he was alone—receded and eventually dissolved in that glumly-rainy morning in this richly-imposing office. The argument, the logic, the rebellion would come later. It would work itself up calmly and cleverly. It was virtually impossible to lead a conversation with Bucky Stander when he sat rustling papers impatiently at a desk which had been constructed from Moby Dick's backbone.

"Let's goose the verities some other time. What did you want to see me about? Or was that it—that you missed the show?"

"No, not quite. I got a phone call last night, about three and a half seconds after you went off the air, from Fat Red himself. Which reminds me. Maybe we'd better begin referring to the old bastard as Redmond. I love and admire him, you understand, but I wouldn't put it past him to hide a tape recorder here under one of the ash trays or something!" Bucky forced a rather patronizing grin as he worried the still-new cigar. "Which means in *Anglaise* that it's fine and dandy for the window cleaners and the copy boys to call him that grammar school name. But we may get in the habit and before we know it we'll be saying it to the window cleaners and the copy boys. And Redmond has the biggest ears since Gable. Or does it sound as though I'm all of a sudden going pompous?"

"Not at all, Bucky. Let's go a step further and turn East and salaam when the thought of him arises."

"Go to hell," Bucky chuckled and sat back, crossing his thick ankles over five dollar Japanese silk hose. "Anyway, the call. I'm sitting on my great duff at ten-thirty last night, finishing up my second pizza pie, and Jeanne's telling me she liked the stripper you interviewed because there were these salient things said about how poor American men are as lovers. You know my Jeanne, how she likes to kid. Then it's Redmond himself on the line, out of the blue."

"A complaint," guessed Jim, recalling that the mostly impromptu interview with Sheila the Shape had wagoned into areas a trace more free-wheeling than he'd meant it to go. "Redmond didn't approve of the talk about sex."

"Oh, nothing like that, not really," Bucky pooh-poohed. "He's not one of your culture vultures, but he's the shrewdest carrot since Barnum; he wouldn't have let her go on if he'd thought she was going to talk about needlepoint and how she tends a rose garden. Call him all the educated names you know, but don't call him a jerk when it comes to commerce."

"Okay. What was the beef?"

"All very polite. He bums incense to you and he still thinks you're the man of the hour; but you're right, the soft-spoken beef was there. He wonders if it had been entirely necessary to goad her into describing in full what the functions of a stripper are. That's one beef."

"'Goad'? Did he honestly use that word in this enlightened day and age? Yes, I know Fat Red. He probably did." Jim sat back. "If you're going to have a stripteaser on a show you don't ask her about how much she enjoyed reading *The Magic Mountain*, it's true. I asked a stripper about stripping the way I'd ask a fisherman about fishing. If she tells me about her job what am I supposed to do, bawl her out? What's the next beef and why didn't he call me personally? I work in his store. I presume he knows the number."

"Come on, kid, don't go prima donna. He called me because he's geared to dealing with representatives." Bucky sat forward a little, with a more winning smile, as if he had agreed to lose a round or two. "Don't go salty. You know the business."

"Sure. Please don't feed the monkeys, elephants or actors. So what's his next beef, Bucky?"

"Well, as I say, he couldn't have been nicer or more soft-voiced. Now you understand I don't agree with him, Jeanne and I think you did a great job, but he did have a slight reservation we can't completely ignore. I mean, constructive criticism is constructive criticism when he signs some of those pretty checks. He sort of thinks that in the future it might be a bright idea to lay low with the—well, let's make up a name for them in a hurry—the low-lifes. The stumblebums of society was the way he put it. You know. The strippers, the grifters, the punks? There's no telling what kind of language they can decide to come up with. I mean I think he's screwy, but maybe he has a sort of a point."

Jim decided it was time to get up. "I have to get back to work, Bucky, so let's drop the manicure. I'm hot stuff this summer because I've broken away from the TV interview that asks the guest about her rose garden. I'm an old news-desk man who's prowling for stories that have some glue to them and the hell with the niceties. That's why the show is looked at as much as it is and that's why I'm going to go on prowling. The minute I go back to the rose garden is the minute we'll all be washing coffee cups at the Automat. Or should I tell all this personally to Big Red? Who, incidentally, is making money out of my show?"

"First of all, take it easy. Remember the Bible. Don't get excited."

"Keep going, Bucky. Tell me about the rose gardens. You have Vittorio Masscino scheduled for *The Hot Spot* tonight. He killed his parents and served thirty years for it. Should I ask him about *his* rose garden? Tell me about all of Mr. Redmond's points, and don't refer to him as anything except Mr. Redmond. He might be listening."

"Aw, lower the voice, Jim, you'll have all the window cleaners in here in a minute," Bucky declared, grinning much too broadly now, his stubby fingers working feverishly. "You know you're set for life. What's the matter? A little criticism burns you up?" The chuckle …

"See you later at the conference, Bucky," Jim said tersely and left the office of violently classy wood paneling and Roman gold humidors.

Walking briskly to his own office, he dredged up the memory of the first thing he could remember Mrs. Wentsmann having said. He had been in the bedroom, changing from his 8 A.M. newscast brown suit to his 6 P.M. newscast blue suit, and he'd overheard her say to Fran, in a voice maniacal in its pride, "… Und I am alzo second cousin to Hermann Goering! You know who iss *Hermann Goering?*" Without meaning to, he had almost abruptly forgotten the incident. Bucky had recommended her because she had worked for over twenty years for Hans Weber

Groeter, who had just written the best seller which had striven to prove that Hitler was the most misunderstood man since Jesus Christ. Jim had listened carefully. He had hired her.

Now he settled at his desk and tried to concentrate on the notes for the noon show. Within minutes Bucky puffed in, wreathed in smiles, with joking apology that wouldn't have fooled a drunk. Bucky reminded him of the party tonight at Monica Enders' penthouse and suggested that he show up. There would be not only plenty of booze and the most imported of anchovies, but Monica, whose cosmetic company sponsored *Jim Creighton's Hot Spot* and who had a vehemently obvious letch for him, had been asking about him.

"Your wife'll be away for a while, won't she?" Bucky hinted. "And Ender may have passed her thirtieth birthday but she can still leave Ava Gardner and Grace Kelly at the starting gate, can't she? I mean, life is life. What've you got to lose? Right?"

"I know about the party, Bucky," Jim said. "Give me a little time. I'll let you know later."

"But …"

The tide had turned so perceptibly that Jim was nearly ready to rub his hands. "I said I'll let you know, Bucky. Right now, let me alone and let me build a noon show, all right?"

Alone, he glanced at his watch and knew that sooner or later she would have to come into the office. On one pretext on another. She would bounce in and tell him that she was ready to stand at attention and salute. Or something.

Three and a half minutes later she did arrive, bringing with her that heady perfume. "Mr. Creighton," she said. "May I see you? Or are you too busy?"

"No," Jim said. "Come in."

CHAPTER THREE

"I MUST BE something of an eager beaver," she declared blandly, coming in with a smile which seemed appropriate, not too forward. She was carrying a neat sheaf of papers. "I wanted to start out bright and early. But there doesn't seem to be anyone in Miss Shoreham's department at all."

Jim half rose. "Do you know it's only twenty past eight?" he notified. "Researchers never get to work at twenty past eight, do they? Even when they're on the job for only two days?"

"They do when they want to keep a job as much as I want to keep this one," she answered, and placed the papers, typed triple-space, on the edge of his desk. "There's some Masscino material here I dug up yesterday and last night. Miss Shoreham gave me a complete briefing about everything, and I'm sure she told me what to do with the copy in the morning. But I'm not overly bright, and I just forgot. Do I bring it here, or wait for her, or what? Or am I stepping out of line by even talking to you this early in the day?"

"Sit down," he offered, waving to the red armchair near his desk, "and we'll have some coffee. Plenty of time to turn the wheels of industry. Cream? Sugar?"

"Black, thanks. No sugar." From the tail of his eye, as he poured coffee from the plug-in-pot on the miniature bar near the door, he noticed that she obediently took the chair and, rather ceremoniously, covered her knees.

"I'm afraid I may have been a little rude—well, in a hurry, let's say—yesterday when Evelyn brought you in here," he said "I didn't mean to be."

"You weren't rude at all. You have probably the most back-breaking schedule in radio and television. You can hardly be expected to shower corn on all the pigeons here at RBS."

He laughed. "Good. Very good," he asserted as he brought her cup to her. "Only please don't mention the word 'corn' anywhere around my enterprises. I'm terribly sensitive." He was reminded again that she couldn't quite be called beautiful (Evelyn was too smart a pro to permit anything like that and, except for that unbelievably wonderful shape, there was no single thing about her that could help to add up to a description of attractiveness. Her teeth were almost blindingly white, but they were a trace too large to have exactly the right proportion to the rest of her face. And although her body looked ripe and eminently healthy, her face was slightly drawn, her cheeks a little too thin.

Yet being this close to her again caused the red flares to go up, to make him begin to understand why he had been so restless for so long.

"Agreed," she nodded, meeting his eyes. "No corn. It slipped out."

"We've established the fact that you're not a prima donna," he said, sitting again, "and that's good, too. I am, once in a while, but only because the past several months have been so hectic. Or that's my current plea, at least. But I'm all Shirley-Temple sweetness after I've blown my top."

"Evelyn ... Miss Shoreham ... told me just the opposite. She said you're the easiest eccentric in the world to work for. Mmm, you cook a mean pot of coffee."

They exchanged several moments of small talk until he feared things were getting faintly out of hand. Nothing that couldn't be rectified speedily enough, but he felt vaguely uneasy. Over the course of only a few minutes or so, he'd handled most of it badly. There was no excuse to be this chummy this early in the game, to give her the we're-all-equals-around-here inference. Not this soon. Her words were probably respectful enough, properly employee-to-boss talk, and from another girl might have sounded even a little groveling. But there was a hair too much certainty about her, an assurance that implied she was prepared to give *him* a few weeks trial here at Rockland Broadcasting. No, he decided, he could have waited another day or two before extending himself. Or at least until he'd had a chance to glance over the way she did research. Sure, Evelyn had done all the initial investigating and interviewing. But Evelyn on occasion had been known to be wrong.

"Uh … in the quickie handshaking yesterday," he said, "all that I heard of your name, unfortunately, was Grant. Miss Grant."

"Mrs. Grant," she amended without the trumpets, without effort or attempts at shaded meanings. "Mrs. Virginia Grant. When it can save time, I'm called Ginny."

Jim nodded, again making a note that she wore no rings, and was sure it was time to switch topics. "Now. Let's see. You say you have some material here on Vittorio Masscino. What's this you said about working last night?"

"Well, again, I kind of feel I may have been stepping out of line. I left the office here and stayed at the Newspaper Library on Twenty-fifth Street until they closed, and went through all the New York papers I could find from May, 1927. That's when he committed the murders. Then I went to the reading room of the library on Forty-second afterwards, because they were open till ten yesterday, and I checked on everything written about him in magazines since 1927. And I went home and typed up that hodge-podge you have on your desk."

"My God," he marveled. "You're not being paid by the hour around here, are you?"

"No, but I got so fascinated, I couldn't stop. It's amazing what you can find about absolutely anything in tattered old magazines. This axe-murder business is old-hat stuff today, I guess, but Masscino, with little school children sending in their pennies and grimy gumdrops to free him, was apparently quite a dramatic figure back in those days. Even as late as 1942 he was having feature articles written about him in everything from *Cosmopolitan* to *Popular Mechanics*."

"My God," he repeated, leafing through the notes.

"What does that mean?"

"Talk about ambition! This looks fine, Ginny. Really fine. We weren't quite planning what they call a banner show upstairs, but some of this stuff—these quotes from his neighbors in Brooklyn Heights, for instance—Hey, this could lead to something exciting." He swung the chair around and raced over the notes. "Just work on that coffee for a minute and keep still."

As she obeyed, his attention was drawn at first to what appeared to be direct quotes *(yes, there were the sources at the bottom of each page, in industrious researcher fashion: The New York Banner Times, The New York American)* from Vittorio Masscino's neighbors in 1927 on Hawthorne Street. Italian and Jewish and Irish and Spanish names, good names, tenement house names, human interest names, and the simplicity with which they talked, so blissfully unaware of syntax, about young Vittorio Masscino, was remarkable—here and there, even poetic. She had thought to copy the entirety of their quotes, lousy but beautiful grammar and all.

"Hey, this could be *really* something!" he enthused, and tossed the paper clip aside as he started from the beginning and read her seven pages of copy. The idea of having Masscino on *Hot*

Spot had been his something like three months ago when he'd read in *The Dispatch* that the gentle little killer was to be released from Sing-Sing. He'd mentioned it as a possibility to Bucky, and the idea had gone back to sleep for at least another month ("Who wants to gawk at a flabby, bald-headed dago who knocked off his parents thirty years ago?" Bucky had shrugged) but Jim had persisted. Now he'd be meeting the man, face to face, at ten o'clock tonight, and this girl had provided him with a gimmick that could deliver the show from the possibly humdrum.

Jim read the copy through, and the new idea crystalized. He lowered the papers to the desk and said, "Get your tennis shoes on, Ginny. You have some work ahead of you."

"I'm ready. What is it?"

"Find out precisely where Masscino lived with his parents on Hawthorne Street in 1927, and go scouting. Do you have a carbon of this copy?"

"Yes. And the other notes I jotted down that I didn't type."

"Good. Then you have the names of the people who came to his defence. Max Greenbaum, Gino Fettilini, that Mrs. Whatzername Giaccopatti. They, especially, because they gave the great quotes. See if they're still alive, still as anxious to talk. See who else is around who'd make good color for an interview along with Masscino tonight. People who knew him from Hawthorne Street, people who went to bat for him."

She as on her feet, obviously as excited by the idea as he. "And when I round them up?"

"Then you phone me. And as soon as you think you've struck pay dirt, we'll pick them up in a cab and deliver them home the same way. With dinner and drinks. None of them will talk about getting money, but if they do, assure them in private they'll be taken care of, and let me know who wants what." He sat back and looked at her, hoping that nothing about the idea would turn harebrained by the time he'd reached for his first luncheon drink this afternoon at Toots Shor's. "Well, how does it sound?" he questioned hopefully. "Nutty? A little too much responsibility for you on the second day of work?"

"It's something straight out of the occult," she said.

"What is?"

"I didn't think of anything approaching this when I went through all those clippings last night, but I admit that something like it struck me when I woke up this morning. This sounds a little insane, I suppose, but I was hoping I'd have an assignment something like this when I came to work. Pardon me if I seem dazzled."

"Dazzle later, Ginny. Just beat it now and phone me the second you hit something."

Evelyn would raise hell, of course, and Bucky Stander would be furious, when they found out that he'd sent a fledgling out on the kind of job they had come to term a mammoth assignment. But somehow it smelled right. Certainly there was nothing to lose, impractical thought or not. If it all meshed by ten tonight, and if the guests sitting across from Vittorio Masscino didn't go all tongue-tied, it could become a show that would please Fat Red. Or even *The Dispatch*'s Steve Lobeck, the only local columnist who had consistently rapped *Hot Spot*.

Although her perfume lingered in the wide office, Jim went back to work. For moments at a time he was able to forget that he was more than ever determined to have her.

"Maybe this is the time for a talk, Jim," said Evelyn Shoreham in his office at eleven-thirty, as he commenced his daily massage. Arnie, RBS' T-shirted masseur with shoulders that flung out to Canarsie at least, had stripped him to his undershorts and had placed him on the portable white slab.

"It's your nickel, Evelyn, but I'm pretty beat," Jim said drowsily as he lay on his stomach and let Arnie pound a few drops of tension out of him. From nine o'clock until ten minutes ago he had read through *The Banner, The American, The Dispatch, The News-Bulletin*, and then had consulted with Clif, and had agreed that the noon newscast, barring fresh emergencies, would shape up okay.

"I don't approve of sending a newcomer into outer-space on a story," Evelyn continued, blasé by now to the fact that she might find him in any state of near undress. Jim had known and worked with Evelyn Shoreham at RBS long before the sudden windfall which had made him the Grand Inquisitor of *Jim Creighton's Hot Spot*, and they had worked well together. As with Monica Enders, the sponsor he was to meet again tonight at her party, there was no positive way of determining Evelyn's age. Ointments, unguents and paints placed her anywhere between thirty-three and forty. She was imposingly dark-complexioned, nearly as tall as he, heavy breasted and with salaciously full lips, and she had never married. Somehow she managed to dress in a fashion far more elegant than was warranted by her weekly salary. Too often she tended to act like a spinster aunt with him, especially when he reached into the hat and pulled out rabbits which might conceivably embarrass the Network and Fat Red, but more than once she had dropped the message that she wouldn't be unwilling to have Jim Creighton share the bed in her snug apartment on Seventy-seventh.

"Grant sounds good to me, Evelyn," Jim replied solemnly as Arnie heroically detached a family of taut nerves from his shoulders. "I told you about her. She brought me what amounts to a perfect outline for a story. Seven triple-spaced pages without a breath of editing needed. Short, concise, to-the-point, and extremely intelligent." He closed his eyes, desperately anxious to relax. "You hired her, didn't you? What're you so excited about?"

"Because she can pitch your name around among the peasants and help to publicize the fact this show is directed from a madhouse. Jim, I'm trying to talk with you! Will you please dismiss this musclebound Armenian and come back to earth?"

"Arnie, you're being called names."

"F'get it, Mr. Creighton," Arnie rasped.

"See, Evelyn?" Jim muttered, lacing his fingers under his jaw. "F'get it. Bawl me out later. I have ten minutes before I have to get dressed for the noon show."

"She's on trial, this Virginia Grant," Evelyn exclaimed. "Sixty-five a week and a credit card at The Spindletop and The Embers. I inherited her from the depths of the research nooks of NBC and Dumont and Columbia. I took her because we needed someone in a rush. I plan to get rid of her in another few days."

"Don't, Evelyn. I like her. She knows what she's doing."

"You like her," Evelyn scoffed. "You like her because of that baby-like swinging rump and that fraudulent smile. Jim, I've been in this business for a lot of years, and I've seen these professional eagers. They start out by owning the corporation; I can sniff them all the way from Baltimore, Maryland. And I can see all your hick-town trust in her, and I'm warning you from all the way over here in right field: you've given her too much to chew all in one Thanksgiving turkey feed. She had no right to plough into your office at dawn and start her tricks, fully aware that I wouldn't show up till late. She knew that, Jim."

"What about the lady from Fairbanks, Alaska? Did you have breakfast with her at The Hampshire House?"

"Yes. And we'll prep her for a five-minute interview on the 6 o'clock show. But …"

"Good."

"Jim, are you listening to me? I had reservations about this Grant girl from the moment she walked in, and now I'm convinced she won't wash. Bucky agrees with me a hundred per cent, but he's too shy to come in here and tell you so."

"Bucky?" Jim asked, momentarily opening his eyes. "Bucky, shy?"

The debate continued—Evelyn becoming more hysterical, Jim becoming more casual—and it ended with Evelyn's decision that she would go back to her office.

Jim and Arnie shared winks.

The remainder of the day, including the noon broadcast, went well. Joe, the Maitre D' at Toots Shor's, summoned him to the phone, where Ginny told him that she had located, talked with and persuaded two of the original defenders of Vittorio Masscino to appear tonight on the show. And if he wanted, there were the kids of the Hawthorne Street neighbors—singled out—who could be available for the price of subway fare to tell what they knew about the Brooklyn Heights legend of Vittorio Masscino.

"Who are the two originals?" Jim asked.

"Giaccopatti and Greenbaum. Greenbaum is old and repeats himself. Mrs. Giaccopatti is full of zip, though. She's Italian and about a hundred, but she has that wonderful Una O'Connor face. She's 'za remember Vittorio like'a from yessaday."

"Good. Get her. Will she come?"

"Will she? I promised her a free dinner at Schrafft's. She loves blueberry pie for dessert."

"Atta girl. Bring her. She sounds as if she'll round it all out. And Ginny thanks."

"Thanks? For what?"

"For the groundwork. Which reminds me. I'm invited to Monica Enders' party tonight. You know her, she pays the bill for our show."

"Oh, yes."

"Will you go with me to it tonight?"

There was the awful pause: "I'm awfully sorry, Mr. Creighton. I have a date tonight. I'm terribly sorry, really."

"Sure."

"But I'll see you there anyway, as a matter of fact That's where my date's taking me."

"Oh? Someone I know?"

"He's a writer named Lee Gardiner. He's sort of a weekend fiance."

"I ... see. I was under the impression you were married."

"I was. My husband died."

".... Oh."

"Thanks again for the invitation. See you later."

CHAPTER FOUR

T HE FOUR O'CLOCK conference on *Hot Spot* in Jim's office was far less comfortable than he recalled its having ever been.

Evelyn, chain-smoking as usual but otherwise giving her effective pose of having all situations well in hand, had just spent a full hour in the pre-interview with Masscino, and now read off the questions she had asked, the questions he had answered and the ones at which he had balked, and gave her always deft summation of the best and the worst that could be expected at air time. Jim, who made a point of never meeting his guest until ten or fifteen minutes before the show, butted in now and then to ask Evelyn to amplify something, or to direct her toward a side of the guest he felt would be of more interest.

Peg Robbins, The Tank's secretary, sat in her usual far-off chair with her skirt resourcefully bunched around her knees, looking dimwitted as usual, but, also as usual, flawlessly getting the meat of the conference on her shorthand pad. In the deep red armchair near the desk slumped Bucky Stander, keeping his conversational distance, chiming in as usual only when he had something cogent and really helpful to say.

For the past five months these late afternoon conferences had sailed along agreeably, without any friction that lasted longer than a couple of minutes. But now Ginny Grant was sitting in Helene Masters' chair directly opposite the desk. She hadn't said a word since the beginning of the meeting; if anything, the way she threw her attention to Evelyn or Bucky or Jim as each of them spoke announced that she was carefully following every word, and going along with every word. There was no way of judging Bucky's opinion of her yet (except for his febrile, cowlicked naughty-boy glances at the exquisite way she was constructed).

But nothing could be more obvious than Evelyn's distaste for her. Evelyn spent the first half of the hour's confab studiously avoiding a glance in the new girl's direction which, of course, offered everyone the chance to cut the air with a cleaver.

"Let's recap," Jim said energetically, joining the game of not looking at Ginny. "People are going to tune in tonight not because a very special murderer named Vittorio Masscino will be there. Young punks today are knocking off their parents with the same casual grace they give to combing their pompadours. And what they've done can be glibly explained away by visiting psychiatrists, brilliant case workers, and a few judges who've read a condensation of Sigmund Freud in *The Reader's Digest.*" He settled back and lighted a cigarette. "So a boy murderer isn't news anymore in our growing civilization, but Vittorio Masscino is. Why? What's so special about Vittorio Masscino?"

"I think," Ginny Grant began, sitting forward, her bright face lighting up.

"Just a moment," Jim interrupted, waving his hand remotely and regarding Evelyn. "You're Sadie Glotz from Tremont Avenue in the Bronx," he baited Evelyn. "You have your choice of viewing *Lineup* or a wrestling match tonight at ten. But you think you'll peek in on Vittorio Masscino instead for five minutes. It's my job to hold you for thirty minutes. What is there about Vittorio Masscino you want to know?"

As always, Evelyn's trigger mind clicked instantly with his and she fell right into character. She lighted a fresh Pall Mall with the burning end of her half-used one, and discreetly crossed her legs. She was considerably more than a handsome young woman,

Jim again reminded himself to remember. On the job she was about as feminine as Broncho Nagurski, good looks and all, but after hours, particularly with the aid of her unspecified, unsaid invitations, she might be worth keeping in mind.

"I remember—or if I don't remember, my folks told me," Evelyn said, mimicking Sadie Glotz, "that thirty years ago a gentle, well-behaved boy named Vittorio Masscino, who loved his mother and father and seven sisters and brothers, and who delivered papers and went to church and was a model kid, found an axe one night and for no reason at all killed his parents. Then he walked to the police station and told them what he'd done, without any show of emotion, one way or another. This is thirty years ago, and I still don't know why he did it."

"Fine," Jim nodded. "Keep going."

"What set this case apart from any of the others was that so many relatives and neighbors came forth to remember something good he'd done, something nice and gentle, such as nursing near-dead birds back to life and never hitting a bully back even though the bully was half his size. And that he was defended in the trial by a dumbbell attorney who acted as if he'd received his law degree only that morning by mail along with a bill for the rent. No one displayed any psychological insight. No one bothered to call in a psychiatrist, a priest or even the family doctor to make a professional comment on him. I wondered why."

Jim nodded briskly. "You wondered why, Mrs. Glotz, because in a way it amounted to the railroading of a semi-innocent. And an extremely likeable semi-innocent, at that. The quick trial, the quick conviction, no rushing for an appeal, the way everyone accepted the decision like dopey sleep-walkers—all of this added up to something you never could quite figure out."

Bucky sat up a little. "And how's about the slew of famous writers and all that yelled like hell for a review of his case?"

"Right," said Jim. "It was a *cause celebre* even more dramatic than Sacco and Vanzetti and Leopold and Loeb, because the hubbub lasted longer. Which means that we want to revive some of that feel of hubbub tonight. Now let's see what we have that can help to do that."

The cushioning segue invited the report from Ginny Grant, and Jim nodded to her. She came through. Offering her report as if she had been a member of Creighton-Stander Enterprises from the beginning, she concentrated on the values of having Masscino's neighbors in the studio, and worked to push home the point that the more rounded-out the image of Masscino, the more effective the show would be.

Through narrowed eyes, Jim spied the bombs subtly drop. Bucky was still regarding her construction and appeared satisfied. Evelyn was the one to watch. Through Ginny's precise set of suggestions, Evelyn's face registered nothing, but her busy, nervous hands were a dead giveaway. You're making this fancy valedictory address because you're making a sprint for the boss, the hands were distinctly saying, and you're going to go about doing your damnedest to take over my job in time. Try it, sister. Try to buck me, You're messing with a pro.

"I understand you okayed the appearances of these neighbors for tonight, Jim," Evelyn said evenly when Ginny had finished.

"Yes," he nodded. "Mrs. Grant tells me that two of them are vocal enough for our purposes. I suggest you put them in seats away from Masscino's and my mikes, but not in the bleachers somewhere. I'll pull them in to the conversation only here and there and try not to give it the rehearsed documentary flavor. We've never tried anything like this before, but even if they phlumph, Masscino's name and the questions you've set up will carry the ball. Sound okay to you, Bucky?"

Bucky shrugged. "I can always throw you the signs from the fishbowl. If they're layin' eggs I can wave for you to use the hatchet."

"Very well, that's the way it'll be," Evelyn intoned abruptly, rising from her chair and stabbing her cigarette into a tray. "I'd better dash back to the office now and round out the interview with the Alaskan dame. She has a small tendency to stutter when she gets excited, Jim, so I'd advise you spend at least twenty minutes with her alone at the mike before the six o'clocker." She took three or four steps toward the door before she turned, ever so easily. "When you're finished here, Mrs. Grant," she added, "would you come back to my office, please?" She went out without waiting for an answer.

Jim paused for a moment, trying to see if Ginny was having any apparent reaction. No, he told himself, none; she had just stepped off the old plantation with vine leaves in her streaming yellow hair and she couldn't have been more trusting of the goodness of radio and television mankind.

"Thanks, Mrs. Grant," he declared soberly. "That'll do it for now. Ah, we have no hard and fast rules about researchers showing up for the actual broadcasts, but you might want to stop by tonight and see how we make our attempts at co-ordination. And, too, the Brooklyn people you rounded up might feel a little more comfortable if they see a familiar face there."

"I'd like very much to come, Mr. Creighton," she replied with another one of those elusive smiles, and in a second was out of the room.

"Well?" Jim asked.

Bucky sloshed around in his chair. "Evelyn's just declared the kind of war that would've made Hitler jealous. I expect to hear gunfire in a couple minutes. You want odds on the champ?"

"I didn't mean that when I said 'Well'," Jim grinned. "What about the girl? You were eyeing her as though you're planning to have her for supper."

"Yeah," Bucky said, clearing his throat, "I see what you mean. The last time I saw a build like that was at Minsky's and my missus wouldn't talk to me for a week. You have plans, kid?"

"Me? Hell, no. You know the rule about mixing business and whatchamacallit. But I'll tell you one thing. That girl knows her stuff. She's two-days old here and she knows exactly what can spark up the show. I'm sold. Helene was a nice, smart gal but she never went out of her way to earn more than sixty-five a week. This one can own RBS in a year if she puts her mind to it."

"Um. That's what I'm kind of afraid of."

"Meaning?"

"Ambition. Ambition that shows a little more than it maybe should. And then again maybe I'm wrong. But that's what Evelyn thinks, and that's what a yokel passing through this office would figure, too. I haven't had a chance to ask Evelyn anything about her. Maybe she's strictly kosher. But I'll tell you better in a week or so." He made a loud, fat man's noise as he got up. "Now I'd better get on my horse and go back to work."

"You have the Evelyn jitters, Bucky. She'll work out fine."

"Oh, I meant to tell you," Bucky informed, putting his cigar into the tray next to Evelyn's mound of cigarette butts. "That Mrs. Wentsmann came by today with this story about your kicking her out on her butt because you were so hard to please, or something. She's in the reception room now, as a matter of fact. I wanted to check with you before I handed her any dough."

"Give it to her. I fired her. I told her to see you."

"Why? After a couple of weeks? What's this all about, you being so hard to please? What're you, getting jumpy all of a sudden? You used to be Tom Sawyer."

"Let it lie, will you, Bucky? Just take care of her and we'll talk about it another time if necessary."

"But …"

"Damn it, you're riding me again!" Jim yelled. "If I'm expected to explain my every move, then let me know now and I'll report in to you every time I want to go to the men's room! Fair enough?"

For certainly the first time in their association, Bucky's face went chalk white. Jim, still seated, held his ground and rustled papers until Bucky lumbered out and let the door close. Outside, the driving rain of the afternoon had once more begun to let up a little.

"Oh, you're making with the primary colors all right, Big Wheel, Jim admonished himself, wishing he had the guts to call Bucky back and apologize for acting like a stereotype of a male starlet. *Nerves,* he tried to assure himself for the dozenth time. *On edge. Jumpy, the way Bucky had said, jumpy the way I've never been jumpy before. A pleasant, friend-to-friend talk begins, and the slightest raising of an eyebrow, the slightest change in friendly tone, and flaring up starts. There no longer was a way to trace any of it. You're a young guy new to the sanctum-sanctorum busy picking the hayseed out of your ears and anxious to receive any bone they want to throw your way, and then without notice you're big time and a word said wrong is enough to make you go haywire. Phone the motivational research houses and find out how long it's supposed to take before you begin kicking shivering mutts and throwing crippled, petrified grandmothers down the cellar stairs.*

Get a hold of yourself, he thought as he struggled to concentrate on the sea of papers in front of him. *Don't get so obvious so damn fast.*

The image of Colter Small came back to plague him. Small had been his English teacher in his senior year at Haylesburg High, and in many ways his closest friend, too; Small had been a scholar of the busy intersection which had included Santayana, Proust and Baudelaire, and he had done his best to infuse Jim with a love for the studious and flexible intellect. "You ought to be satisfied with your native intelligence and charm, Jim," Small had told him, "but it's clear you're not. You pretend you're ambitious, too. You aren't, you know, not really. Why in the world should you let yourself get involved in a world you're simply not constituted to make, when you show no honest signs of even wanting to make it?"

Nerves, Jim thought now. *I'll make it up to Bucky in some way. He won't stay sore. I'm not even sure he's sore at all. He has one talent I never had. He can let an insult roll off his back without going to pieces. Sure. It'll all work out. I'll find a way to laugh it up, and it'll all work out.*

It's got to.

RBS' afternoon recorded music show, *Disk Doctor*, was being piped into her office as Evelyn Shoreham returned to it and allowed the door to slam behind her. Flanders Bryce Redmond had permitted her and the other wage slaves one out, to tune the record jockey either up to loud or down to soft, and she tuned it as softly as it could go and still be an integral part of The System. *Dear 1984, old lover*, she thought bitterly, *come and ravish me. I'm yours.*

The Grant bitch with the sexy-red lower lip and the wildest body this side of stag shows would have to go, and soon. That was for quadruple sure. You could work for men efficiently and with the kind of round-the-clock pace that defied the stopwatch, and one over-eager bitch with a bust-line that did better than match yours could come along and crumb it all up.

Unless you were on your guard. Unless you knew constantly that only Number One counts.

"I know it's unprofessional and everything else you say," Helen Masters had twittered right here in the office, "but I have to leave. I love Bert and we want to get married right away and he won't take no for an answer and his parents are waiting for us in New Haven and I'm a little bit pregnant, Evelyn, and I'm sorry but I'll have to leave. You can understand."

Evelyn Shoreham, who knew how good she was as a researcher, would have been willing to have taken over all the research operations for *Hot Spot* herself, if Stander hadn't ordered her to get a substitute in a hurry. She had accepted the Grant girl only because the word had spread around the meaningful booths at The Absinthe House and Shor's and Clark's that the Grant girl was bright and quick.

Lighting a cigarette now as she waited for the girl to knock at her door, Evelyn remembered who had made the oversized recommendations. A wolfpack of radio and TV men, producers, directors, and public relations men, who surely must have slept with her. Evelyn had met the type, and discovered herself beating her fists against her desk when she realized that it had been she, and no one else, who had welcomed a grasping whore into the organization. Bucky Stander would snap her garter somewhere between lunch and dinner, and Jim Creighton, whose brain equalled that of the little boy who delivered the Kleenex, would be giving her the rush act within the first few hours.

"Miss Shoreham?" the voice sounded suddenly as the door opened. "You wanted to see me?"

"Yes. Come in. Close the door."

Evelyn faced her, waited only a beat until the kid had advanced a step and then offered no invitation to spar. "I was under the impression for a while yesterday, Mrs. Grant, that we were going to work well together."

Virginia Grant blinked, sat on the hard backed chair and primly laced her fingers over her knees. "So was I, Miss Shoreham. Is there any reason why we can't?"

So she's going to play the Who? Me? part, thought Evelyn truculently. "It seems you were the one who thought not. I'm willing to concede that I wasn't quite explicit enough yesterday with the fact that you work for Mr. Creighton and Mr. Stander, but through me only. One of the reasons I'm employed here is to keep all trivia off Mr. Creighton's and Mr. Stander's burdened shoulders. Marching into Mr. Creighton's office this morning, when I made it reasonably plain that ..."

She was holding her own; looking childlike and ready to be thrashed, but nevertheless holding her own. "Excuse me, Miss Shoreham. I don't mean to talk out of turn and I'll do as I'm told from now on. But neither Mr. Creighton nor Mr. Stander thought that what I did was trivia."

"That's quite beside the point."

"How is it? I realize I've just started this job, but I want the show to be as successful as you do. Truly."

It wasn't going the way it was supposed to. "All right then, let's try to have an understanding," Evelyn asserted, feigning a brief smile they both recognized as a phony. "And let's clear it up now before we begin swapping subtleties that can't help at all. You did this morning what you imagined to be a shrewd thing. You purposely went over my head to the bossman who's impressed by pretty young girls with industry. What you may not know is—"

"Just a moment, Miss Shoreham—"

"No, you wait a moment, Mrs. Grant," Evelyn cut in, biting down hard on the Mrs. "I can read your great big planned dream as plainly as if it were printed on your forehead. You want to run this circus and maybe even cop a few other honors, too. But it isn't going to work. A few other glorified clerks in this outfit, with twice your equipment, had the same big dazzling plan, and they're back selling hosiery at Macy's bargain counter."

Quit your job, damn it, you ambitious little bitch! Evelyn silently pleaded. *Have the guts to stand up and punch me in the nose and tell me you're quitting!*

"You're a little more upset than the situation seems to call for, aren't you, Miss Shoreham?" said Virginia Grant smoothly. "I have nothing against you. I haven't the least desire to fight with you. If I've made a mistake, and you can persuade me it was a mistake, I'll be perfectly willing to see that it never happens again. But I can't very well give an inch if you don't give an inch, too, can I?"

The obstinate little fool was smiling at her!

Slow down, Evelyn told herself as she retreated to her desk and felt the panic start to rise. *Whatever you do, no hysterics. No noise. No impression that suggests a contest.* "I see," she found the contained voice to say, "that you've been in this position before. You have all the answers so ready at hand."

"No. I simply said what I felt."

"All right, then, I'll tell you what I know. Then you can go for the day because I'm swamped with work. And you can paste this piece of advice in your hat for reference over the weekend. I've seen your kind in action many times, and it's fairly obvious that you intend to keep batting those eyelashes for Creighton. So listen well, Mrs. Grant, you'll get away with your tricks once more, maybe even two or three times more, but then you're going to do something to really rile me, and I'm going to pull the oldest line in the history of business. You know what I'm going to say?"

"No."

"I'm going to say, 'Either she goes or I go.' And you know what'll happen? The reverse of the old gag. You'll go, Mrs. Grant, because you fill out a bathing suit better than I do and you may be a whingding between the sheets, but I make this organization succeed as well as it succeeds. And both Mr. Stander and Mr. Creighton know this better than they know their wives' names."

"Miss Shoreham—"

"I'm not finished," Evelyn blustered, and damned herself for bringing personalities into the issue, the one thing she had sworn she would never do. "There's a cozy little blacklist around this industry, Mrs. Grant. I don't mean the one with the subversives on it. I mean the one that mentions the over-eager little Wellesley or Smith graduates like you, Mrs. Grant, the little helpers who cause trouble wherever they go. Maybe you see me as a cantankerous old biddy, Mrs. Grant, and maybe I am. But I'm more than that. I'm the gal behind those famous scenes that everyone in this business knows. And I can put you on that little list so fast that your head won't stop spinning for a year. I hope you're not crazy enough to doubt it."

"Well, I'm not crazy, Miss Shoreham, if that's what you're asking," she replied with the same simplicity one would employ to talk about a reasonably painless headache. She kept looking at Evelyn, but the sign was up that she wasn't intending to say anything more.

"What else do you want to say?" Evelyn offered.

"Nothing at all," she answered without any apparent guile. "I work for you, and I'd like to go on working for you and the show. I told you before. I have no desire to fight."

A phone buzz from Gladys at the reception room mercifully broke the immediate tension. "That's all, Mrs. Grant," Evelyn said crisply. "I'll see you here on Monday morning."

"All right," the girl nodded sweetly, the model of mature composure as she rose from the chair and went out of the office. The smiling exit pretended that the two of them had been whiling away the nerve-end of a rainy July afternoon, talking about the perils of Mah-jong and whether or not they could get away with serving their men only corned beef hash for dinner tonight.

This one couldn't be scared off, Evelyn knew as she began the day's third pack of cigarettes. Jim's complicatedly clumsy little wife was away for the summer, and he was understandably contemplating his navel and deciding that he was God's gift to the world. The way he'd gawked at the Grant girl had been as subtle as an elephant's gas. He was a handsome dumb yuk with no more talent than at least seventy-five other radio men in New York had, but he had hit the jackpot and it would be like successfully striking a match against a cake of soap to unseat him.

And meanwhile, back at the libido, he would have a remarkable pair of breasts named Virginia Grant to give him the soothing balm, to dish out the mushy stuff, and soon enough to stick a ring in his nose and let him know that the two most evil words of the decade since Joseph Stalin were Evelyn Shoreham. It was a horrible business, when you had the courage to really look at it. A genuinely good network of skills were, in the long run, no lasting match for a still-ripe pair of breasts.

Pretty soon it would have to happen. She, Evelyn Shoreham, whose office walls were lined with the affectionately autographed photographs of Godfrey, Berke, and all the original kingpins of television, would be let go. Maybe not from Stander-Creighton. Maybe the old-hat bluff would work with Grant and all the certain Grants to come, and she would keep her cushy job with Rockland Broadcasting even after Jim Creighton was toppled, as he and Bucklin Stander would most positively be in time. Maybe she would be moved onto another enterprise, where she did all the work, and the bulging biceps and gleaming teeth got all the reviews in the trade papers. But she was approaching forty and, more quickly than she would have thought, she was commencing to screech when she wanted to express herself. And wasn't it a matter of practical policy to play up a lush youngster at the helm, a beauty with Instant Brain, who could deal with all oppressive problems by showing just a trifle more thigh? Doom doom doom, sure. But that was the way the coaxial crumbled.

I won't knuckle, she thought resolutely. *If it involves hiding efficiency and making like a cat in heat with Jim Creighton, then that's how it will be. I gave up the practice of adding sex to my repertoire of skills in business long ago.*

Maybe now's the time to revive it.

In her own calculating way, Virginia Grant is ahead of the game. She has a lot more than I have to offer Jim Creighton. But the 'more' consists of quickie fluff. If it's true that sex is the weapon that keeps you above water, then hold this bra for me, seconds, and stand back. I'm diving into the pool, and I'll win the meet because I'm fighting for my life.

CHAPTER FIVE

THE MASSCINO SHOW came off perfectly. Even Bucky, Evelyn and Ginny Grant in the fishbowl, the glassed-in room directly opposite the microphones in Studio D, seemed to sense how smoothly it moved from the beginning. Masscino, a short, balding, bulky man, had been nervous for only a moment. But once eased by Jim just before air time, the apprehension had fled, and he answered every question put to him, intelligently and unhesitatingly.

His brother and sister-in-law, who had accompanied him to the studio, had appeared suspicious of everything, and Evelyn had spent a cheerless minute or two in keeping them settled at the far corner of the room. Mr. Greenbaum and Mrs. Giaccopatti proved to be magnificent guests, responsive and unrambling.

It was one of the top ones, Jim decided, and more than once he found himself instinctively looking towards Ginny.

Hardly a minute after he'd given the last Monica Enders commercial and wrapped up the show, Bucky waddled in to announce that the WRBS switchboard had been active from 10:05 on, and the bulletins had been phoned in to him in the fishbowl. People were jamming the station with offers of jobs for Masscino. "You check with a Miss Harvey in Room two-ten on your way out," he advised Masscino, "and she'll relay the messages that've come in so far. Leave your phone number or where you can be reached by her, and by tomorrow she'll contact you with the rest of the calls. That fast enough action for you, kid?"

"Mister, I—I don't know what to say …" Masscino muttered huskily, his eyes brimming with tears, his attention ping-ponging from Jim to Bucky and back to Jim again. "You all treated me so good, I …"

"We want to thank you, Mr. Masscino," Jim said and shook his hand. "And your friends here, too. It was a fine show." He noticed Ginny leaving the fishbowl and he said, "Uh—excuse me." He left the studio and tried to reach her without fueling a new fight with Evelyn. Evelyn, busy at the telephones, didn't seem to notice.

Ginny Grant was in the corridor, pressing the elevator button. She appeared neither overjoyed nor surprised to see him advance toward her.

"Congratulations, Mr. Creighton," she greeted. "It went like greased lightning tonight. It was warm and human without once being maudlin." She wore a transparent yellow raincoat over a simple but low-cut peasant blouse and a precisely pleated gray skirt. Her hair was pulled back in a pony tail. She looked seventeen.

"Can I drop you somewhere?"

"Thanks. It isn't necessary. I can get a subway right around the corner and be home in ten minutes."

"Where do you live?"

"The Village. Cornelia Street."

Towering over her in the otherwise vacant corridor, trying to make conversation that would start the sparks flying, he felt foolish and gangling. "That's my old stomping ground. Or just about. I lived in a rabbit-warren on Bleecker for six years after the War."

"Sure, I know Bleecker. Was Frijole Joe's in business when you lived there? I ate something Spanish there once and the roof of my mouth was numb for two weeks."

"Spanish food on Bleecker? Can't be! That's like finding knockwurst in Chinatown. Uh …"

"Jim," Evelyn Shoreham had called coolly from behind. "Mr. Stander and I will be in his office when you're ready."

The elevator door opened and Ginny smiled as she stepped in. "See you later, Mr. Creighton."

In his semi-sumptuous office, Bucky performed a nightly ritual. He poured three massive slugs of Scotch for himself, Evelyn and Jim, and passed them around with the same pride of sharing that a newly-ordained pastor exhibits in passing new hymnals around. The three relaxed, sipped and, for the first minute, said nothing. There was nothing to suggest that any of them had exchanged an unpleasant word with each other during the arduous day. The rain had resumed, the lights were purposely low and restful, and they were simply three hard-working people who seemed basically to be fond of one another.

"Today was a dandy dilly, I'll tell you that," Bucky remarked happily. "Masscino came across like he's been at a mike all his life. And the Greenbaum guy and the old lady, you handled them like peaches and cream, too. If Redmond caught it tonight, I'll bet my last dime he went nuts over it." He sipped sparingly. "Even the six o'clocker was a doosy. That Alaska dame could get a show of her own."

"Give Evelyn all the credit for that one," Jim maintained, awkwardly aware that Evelyn, sitting between them, was unusually moody, even morose. She had finished her drink, and was liberally pouring another—something neither Jim nor Bucky had ever seen her do before. "The script was her baby from start to finish."

"It was nothing," Evelyn disclaimed drily.

Bucky, who was never the most sensitive member of the organization, noticed the moodiness, and exchanged a questioning glance with Jim. A bit too ostentatiously, he recrossed his fat legs, cleared his throat, and drastically changed the subject He suggested they run down the list of the next week's guests quickly; then he'd have to beat it and pick up his wife for the Enders' party. Evelyn came to a little, lighted another cigarette, and reminded them that the upcoming Thursday night slot was still not completely nailed down. A lieutenant from the old America First movement had promised to appear, but his daughter had phoned this afternoon to say he'd come down with the flu and might or might not be available for Thursday. "I'll dream up a standby over the weekend," Evelyn promised.

"Aw, it'll turn out," Bucky assured. He set his unfinished drink on his desk and got up. "Right now, Uncle Bucky is bushed. I'm gonna show up at Enders' blowout just to put in an appearance, and then go home. My sinuses start raising holy hell when we get weather like this. I still may drop this whole racket and move to Honolulu." He picked up his hat and began to waddle toward the door. "You kiddies cornin'?"

"We'll go in a minute or so, Bucky," Evelyn said, speaking for herself and Jim. "Have a nice time."

"Yeah. You'll show up later, won't you, Jim?"

"Sure, Bucky."

"Evelyn? You be there?"

"I—doubt it. My desk at home is piled high with work. I imagine Enders can survive my not coming."

"Well, all work and no play, I always say. So long, kids."

Jim surveyed her as Bucky went out. Not looking at him, she downed the second drink and rose tiredly from her chair to reach for the neck of the bottle.

"Give me your glass," she said softly. "Nobody with sense nurses a drink on a Friday night after a rough week."

"Maybe one more," he said. "I don't want to show up stoned."

He watched her pour the Scotch carelessly, aimlessly into his glass but he kept quiet. She handed it to him, still keeping her eyes averted.

"This is sort of new for you, isn't it?" he asked. "You usually have one and then hardly even touch it. You had a good dinner, I hope."

"I had a grilled cheese sandwich and a container of coffee at four-thirty," she replied tonelessly and refilled her glass. "About two or three times in my life I've conscientiously, deliberately tried to get myself drunk. But it never really happened. Then I read somewhere that it's easy as pie if you drink on an empty stomach. The other two or three times I was full of food. Or full of something." She raised her glass. "Well, as they used to say at the scandal magazines, here's mud in your eye."

"What gives, Evelyn?"

"What gives how? Who?" she frowned, sitting again, this time without her usual flare for impeccable grace.

"What's eating you?"

"Oh, drop it. Nothing's eating me. I just feel like being a little brittle and nasty tonight. You know, the teetotaler who gets loaded and becomes a raucous bore and doesn't even know or care that she's become one. You can go if you like."

"And I can repeat the question. What's eating you?"

"I told you there's nothing."

"And I can say one other thing, Ev. You can be an awful pain in the neck sometimes, but I've never known you to be evasive or bitchy for the sole purpose of being bitchy. I like you and I respect you, so I'm asking it straight: What hurts?"

Evelyn peered at her cigarette reflectively and then, for the first time, looked at him squarely. "Bucky tells me that Fran went out of town yesterday for a vacation. How long will she be gone?"

"We're not sure yet. Maybe the summer if I keep this busy. She feels in the way, I guess."

"What'll you do about eating? Grab Nedick hot dogs on the run? That's what men usually do when they're not looked after."

Jim paused, afraid of what was to come next; she was leaning too hard to make him escape without something of a scene. "I used to get my best nourishment from Nedick hot dogs," he answered with forced lightness.

"I have an offer to make," she said flatly, almost sullenly. She had taken another unsparing sip and was now glaring at the wall ahead of her. "I have a steak at home, and last Christmas I got three bottles of champagne that haven't been opened. I cook a good steak and I'd promise not to talk shop once."

He searched for a quick answer to give her. There had to be an unslick and painless sentence he could speak that would tell her he knew what she was offering him and that there were at least a dozen reasons why he couldn't accept it now.

The air conditioned paneled office was sharply oppressive as she seemed to be both urging an immediate reaction from him and wishing that she could swiftly retract what she had said. "You're there, aren't you?" she asked in a risky monotone, still frowning at the wall. "You heard me?"

"I did, Evelyn. Yes."

"And you're saying no."

"With reasons. Believe me, Evelyn, with reasons."

"I'll offer it again, once more, just once more, if it's a matter of salesmanship. When I was one and twenty, I was famous for salesmanship." Her handsome face was creased in a hot-but-controlled anger she couldn't disguise. The semi-backtracking, by way of dank humor, made all of it ugly. "I'm not asking you for anything that will last through next year. I'm asking you for something as simple as the directions to the Independent Subway."

"I'm sorry, Evelyn."

"Good. You're sorry. You're sorry about what? That I insulted you by telling you I want to sleep with you tonight?"

He waited for more. He waited for her turn again to look at him. He waited for himself to get up and go to her, to touch her not in desire, not in there-there paternalism, but with some lucid message that might let her know that he understood the embarrassment, the terrible embarrassment she must surely be feeling. But she was waiting for him to take over.

"I'm sorry you thought you had to get looped to say it to me," he asserted, and then instantly recognized that it had been the worst thing he could have uttered.

Evelyn did turn toward him, then, her slate-colored eyes now two burnt coals of fury. She lifted the half-filled glass of Scotch and, with only a second's hesitation, hurled its contents into his face.

"You what, you pompous bastard?" she screamed. "You *what?* Love? Is that what you talking about? *Love?* Shame about hiding feelings? What's the other pompous word: torch? You think all this happened because I *love* you?" She was on her feet then, weaving ever so slightly, and for an instant he imagined she was going to find something else to throw at him. "You cruddy, self-satisfied, overbearing success."

"Ev …" he said hoarsely, helplessly.

"Ev' what? Quiet down? Making too much noise? Will the cleaning women find out that the great Jim Creighton is involved in something unpleasant? You dumb, fat, happy slob with all the sudden success … what were you doing a few years ago, selling ties for a buck an hour? Don't get patronizing with *me*, big man. You know where you'll be a year from now, even with all the money and contracts and the hundred-dollar whores that let you have it for free because you're Creighton? A year from now you're going to be washed up because no ninety-day wonder like you lasts longer than a year. Winchell and Kilgallen'll say you've bought that ranch in Arizona to give you time to come up with new TV plans, but that'll be double talk. What it means is that you'll be on your backside, you big, smug success, you, and at The Harwyn and Twenty-One they'll still bow and scrape, but you'll know you're out. And then sooner than you think, you'll be back selling those ties."

Redmond's plan for an all-encompassing piping-in of WRBS radio was still in effect. From Bucky's Hi-Fi, off near the office bar, Gil Harper was giving a five-minute news summary.

Suddenly, Evelyn was standing still, and she was silent. There was the faintest indication that she knew she'd said far too much to the man who could bounce her out of Rockland Broadcasting. She eyed him, waiting for even the slightest reaction.

Get her out, he thought instinctively. *Tell her she's been bounced, with the same ease it took to bounce Mrs. Wentsmann. The Miracle Men upstairs won't even raise their eyebrows. Good worker, but unstable. Querulous with the wrong people at the wrong times. Not part of the team. He could work it, and no one, not even Bucky, could raise a successful stink.*

"I think I've done my Bette Davis stint for the day," Evelyn said wearily. "I'm going home now. I'll phone in for all the severance pay rules on Monday morning."

"Sit down, Ev," Jim directed, still attempting to swab the Scotch from his hair and collar with a gracefulness he didn't have. "It's my turn to apologize because you misunderstood me. Sit down."

"Oh, drop it. I'm going home and I meant it. At this point, I'm so gawddamn sick of the toadying I've done for the past twenty years that I want to puke. Which, as a matter of fact, I'm about ready to do, anyway. Good night, Mr. Creighton, and don't do country-bumpkin things like insisting I stay and kick empty words around when I have no intention of doing so."

Jim watched her leave, with a carriage that had considerably more sobriety than she'd shown a few minutes before.

Alone in Bucky's office he drained his drink and itched for another, although he remembered that he was expected to show up tonight cold sober. Bucky had told him so. Appearances. Only the trade would be there. But only two things counted to get you rich: a good baritone voice, and appearances.

Her words had hit home with such impact that it would have been suicide to face them and minutely examine them. Instead, he switched off the small light, closed Bucky's office, and tipped fifty cents when the doorman found him a cab. He rode home, reshaved and reshowered, changed his clothes, and decided it was much too late to telephone Fran at Cabott Island. The telephone answering service detailed the eight calls that had come in through the day, but none of them warranted a speedy call-back. He debated about having a quickie drink at Tim Costello's before taxiing to the party, but feared that Ginny Grant might get there before him, and leave. He built a double bourbon on the rocks and sipped at it as he worked at the cuff links and the Windsor knot.

Drunk or sober, Evelyn Shoreham's wrong, he assured his image at the full-length mirror before he stepped out of the apartment. *You'll still be around in a year. You'll be bigger than ever. Everyone says so. You say so. Fran says so, Bucky says so, your fans say so. Even the bourbon says so. The good, expensive bourbon.*

"Taxi!" called the doorman in front of the apartment building as he emerged. "Taxi for Mr. Creighton!"

CHAPTER SIX

JIM ENTERED MONICA ENDER's apartment house lobby on the Fifth Avenue side of Central Park South at a little after midnight. He had brought Fran here to a party of hers in March, just after Enders had signed to sponsor *Hot Spot*. It had been a large, noisy, rather witless and too-quickly drunken party, and he imagined tonight's would be a duplication.

"Penthouse, please," he said now.

"Yes sir. Uh, begging pardon, sir," the operator said in a moment. "But aren't you John Creighton?"

"That's right," said Jim Creighton.

"I watch your program every chance I get."

"Thank you very much."

The contract-signing party had enthralled Fran, who'd bumped into a celebrity every time she'd turned around. With the two rye and ginger ales which she'd nursed through the evening, she'd enjoyed every minute of it. She had danced once with Guy Landis, whose movie she'd seen just that afternoon at the Paramount. She had been pinched at least once by a get-rich-quick Broadway director whom Jim later in the kitchen had quietly warned to cut it out. She had remembered, perhaps a bit too unnecessarily, to tell the hostess that she had been using the Monica Enders lipsticks for years. Jim had drunk considerably more than two drinks that night, but he had left the party, with his wife, as sober as a Flanders Bryce Redmond.

"Take it slow with the sauce," Bucky had advised him. "Drink up whenever she sashays by and worries about your glass, but teach yourself the science of nursing. The first way to get us shown the door in this racket is to be known as a bright boy who can't hold the sauce. And don't look at the piano player when she accidentally leans over in her famous low-cutters and accidentally on purpose shows you what separates the men from the boys. Romance her, keed. Don't drag her off to the veranda, but romance her. Sure insurance against option jitters."

Tonight's party was going strong as he stepped out of the elevator onto the eighteenth floor and heard the deafening merge of hypertonic voices from the penthouse above. Sighing, he mounted the single flight, gave his name to a starched butler, and was admitted to the empire of Monica Enders.

"Darling, you're on time!" she cried, flying from the outer space of a living room that made his own look like a condemned shack, and nearly suffocating him with the powerhouse of what he had come to recognize as her own make of perfume. "And you're alone. How dreadful! Or should I say how marvelous? Where is your-uh-delightful wife?"

"Fran's away for a little while, Mrs. Enders. Out of town."

"Oh?" she preened as she lifted her pretty cheek to be kissed, in a motion that was so noticeably oversexed that it became both sexless and vulgar. "Well, I'm old enough to have heard all those deliciously disgusting things about what mice do in the summer while the cat goes to Martha's Vineyard, or wherever it is that cats go for the summer. Come," she commanded, taking his hand and squeezing it. "Let me take you inside and feed you to the wolves. Or wait a sec. What's the female counterpart of wolf? Maybe you'd better not ask, at that. And for God's sake, if you *ever* call me *Mrs.* Enders again, I'll slit your gorgeous throat. The name is Monica."

Jim let himself be steered into the arena, grabbing a cocktail from a passing tray as he went, and struggled to stop looking glum. For one thing, there was Bucky, all tuxedoed-out and making brittle, probably cogent, but business-sexified conversation with one of those advertising agency camp followers with a bosom, who has no immediately-recognizable role in the scheme of things, but who might any day turn out to be the lady who can help to slit your throat.

For another, there was no complex reason to be antagonistic to Monica Enders, sponsor or no sponsor. She gushed a lot, sure, and there was something concentratedly and even proudly empty-headed about her. But there was nothing hostile or even questioning in her still-lovely face, nothing that signalled he should dislike her simply because Bucky pandered to her. Her striking figure was only three or four years away from being a teenager's figure and there was no doubt about her instinctive class. She was either in her late thirties or late forties; there was no noble way to gauge, and if her burnished hair and arresting face were toyed with, with Monica Enders Products, again there was no way to tell. There had been no talks on the subject, of course, but the clearest announcement he had heard in his life was that she was determined to go to bed with him. And what, he thought, was there about that bit of news to make him hostile?

Her elaborate front room was filled, seemingly far beyond capacity, with most of the well-barbered or well-Helena Rubensteined faces he had noticed at party after party like this one:

The overdressed dowager who had knocked them dead in *The Little Foxes* in Cleveland and then had gone on to marry someone whose name was not dissimilar to Gottrox.

The underdressed starlet who undulated from man to man and who was only too willing to shack up with anyone who could get her starred at The Copa or The Latin Quarter.

Three newspaper columnists, with illiterate prose styles, who would be back at the rewrite desks if the city's press-agents dosed up shops tomorrow morning.

Bucky's twittering wife, who loved to be told by shampooed men half her age that she looked half her age.

Bruce Cavanaugh, the marcelled dandy who was Flanders Bryce Redmond's right-hand hatchet, and his highly polished woman.

Four commercial prostitutes and their dates.

Two prostitution applicants and their dates.

At least six dozen show business hangers on—advisors, managers, agents, counsellors, professional no-talents.

And the pianist was getting industrious with Gershwin's Rhapsody. The white coats at the bar were pouring drinks at a wild pace. The carvers at the roast beef table would, in another time, have been cutting off heads at *La Place De Vendome*. One of the prostitute applicants was doing an awkward, inappropriate Cha-Cha as she bared her ankles and loudly begged the bored pianist to play *Ain't We Got Fun*.

He polished off the first cocktail almost before he knew it and had begun on his second when Monica Enders clutched at his arm, lugged him off to perhaps the only open spot in the overly-populated room, and told him she'd been waiting for a chance to have a talk with him alone. The waiters kept threading through with red caviar and frankfurters the size of a thumb.

Then the din lowered a little, as though by pre-arrangement, and suddenly he saw Ginny Grant in the direct center of the room.

She was standing there, with that wonderful carriage, accepting a drink from what had to be the man who had brought her. He was a muscular young man with all the innate masculinity of a calla lilly.

Once she looked up and across the busy room.

She saw him. She smiled sweetly.

"That fellow looks familiar," Jim told Monica Enders, surreptitiously pointing to Ginny Grant's date. "Is he the one you invited, or the girl?"

"Who? Let me see." Her eyes narrowed and crinkled; Monica could barely see two feet in front of her, the backstairs gossip went, but she steadfastly refused to wear glasses. "Oh. Lee Gardiner. Yes, I've been inviting him to these picnics for two years now, although he doesn't work for the firm anymore. An extremely talented boy. It's tragic how he went to seed."

"Should I know of him?"

"You do, don't you? Lee Gardiner? He wrote that beautiful book, *Pelican Street*, that absolutely everyone was reading several years ago. He was going to be the next Thomas Wolfe, but he never wrote another word. Except for the firm. One of our vice-presidents heard he was available and talked the agency into letting him write some face-powder copy. He did it quite well for a while, I was told, and then he became unreliable. Naturally, he had to be let go." Monica bit her lower lip tentatively and then pulled an invisible thread from his jacket sleeve. "Jim, darling, I have a dreadful confession to make. I wasn't able to watch your show tonight, and I've heard from just everyone that it was marvelous!"

"Thanks. It did go quite ..." Jim fumbled, unable to take his eyes off Ginny. Fortunately they were interrupted by the Cleveland dowager who broke into the conversation and began one of her own. Monica introduced them, Jim nodded stiffly, and excused himself. Through the dense clusters of guests he made his way to Ginny.

She was alone. Her dark cocktail dress clung tightly to her preposterously perfect body, and dipped in coyly at the navel without seeming flashy or fisheye-catching.

"Hello, again," she greeted, and her smile was warm and intimate, for him only.

"I didn't see you come in," said Jim.

"I make a very unobtrusive entrance."

"Suppose we make an unobtrusive exit. Right now."

Her eyebrows lifted. "Oh?" she asked, not understanding, not misunderstanding. There was, he realized once more, no sure way of ever judging what her words or face really meant to convey. "You mean now? Right here and now?"

"I mean right here and now. No one will miss us."

"And where will we go?"

"Anywhere away from here. Can you ditch your date without too much trouble?"

"Well, I suppose I could, but ..." she began, still smiling, apparently not taking him too seriously. But then the muscleman swooped back, carrying two glasses.

"Excuse intrusion," he interrupted genially. "Here's your medicine, Virginia. As the doctor ordered. One Stinger for you, a ginger-ale for me." He was not so tall as Jim, but he was solidly, athletically built, with the type of post-Dorian Gray face which has just commenced to exhibit the signs of dissipation.

"Thank you, Lee," she acknowledged, accepting it and slipping her free hand under his arm, in an abrupt show of fond possessiveness which Jim didn't believe for a moment. "Lee, I'd like you to meet Mr. Creighton. Mr. Creighton, may I introduce Lee Gardiner. One of the four or five best authors in America today."

"Glad to meet you," Lee Gardiner exclaimed, crushing Jim's hand. "Reason I'm on the ginger-ale kick is that I'm on the wagon with a vengeance. Thanks to Ginnypoo here, I've been off the hard stuff for six and a half days now and I feel like I could lick Gene Tunney in his prime. Great little gal, Virginia."

"Oh, cut it out, Lee," she said, obviously amused. "Will you be a doll and get Mr. Creighton a drink?"

"In a flash," Gardiner enthused. "What's your poison, Mr. Creighton?"

"Uh—Scotch, please. Rocks and an eyedropper of water."

"Coming up. That's the smart man's drink. They say if a man sticks to Scotch, he'll never become a lush. Me, I was strictly a gin man, myself. Wait here and I'll be right back."

Jim blinked at her for a moment. "That's really your fiance, Ginnypoo?"

"Don't talk that way," she said. "He's kind of Young Dog Tray, but he's really nice. And he's having a fierce time keeping away from alcohol. I think he's going to make it, though."

"We were talking before about cutting out together. And you were about to say something."

"I would like to leave with you. I mean that," she replied evenly, for the first time letting him know with her candid eyes that she knew precisely who he was, and precisely what he wanted. "But I'd never come to a party with one man and leave with another. I know that's standard accepted procedure these days, but I'm the last holdout. I bake Girl Scout cookies and read *Little Women*."

"Let me call you, then."

"Fine," she smiled, and without the least dramatic flourish recited her telephone number.

Wally Brunow, a bushy-haired, backslapping, swell guy who had been directing a successful comedy series for one of the largest networks for a half dozen years without losing his own sense of humor, sidled up a minute before Jim expected Gardiner's ebullient return. "Well, whaddaya know!" Wally cried, punching Jim's shoulder and kissing Ginny's cheek. "My two oldest and dearest friends! Jim, still a dour son of a bitch, I see. And Ginny, sexy as ever. Sexier."

Jim greeted him, and was a little surprised to see that Ginny appeared to know him so well, too. "Hello, Wally," she responded. "How nice to see you."

"Hey, I heard the scoop," Wally ventured. "That you two rasslers are workin' together now, as of when—yesterday? Jim, you just died and went to Heaven. Ginny Grant's the greatest helper-outer any harassed old bastard in television ever had. Honey, if he and Stander don't start payin' you a grand a week by next Friday, come to me and I'll have him called up before the ASPCA or something. Hey, I've been here ninety whole seconds and no one's offered me any hooch! I think I'll take up *that* grievance before the ASPCA first. Excuse me. I see a St. Bernard over yonder to help me out. Looks like my sponsor's wife. See you later." Wally hurried off, clapping backs and kissing cheeks as he went.

"Wally isn't ready to join the Shrinking Violet League, is he?" Ginny said, delicately bringing the Stinger to her full, coral lips. "He's about the only man in the business who doesn't have an enemy waiting with a stiletto."

"He's a great fellow," Jim nodded. "But you're a little hard on a few others in the trade, aren't you? Not everyone in town is brandishing a knife."

"Oh, not brandishing. No one ever raises his voice. This is the slyest, coolest profession on the face of the earth. Everybody worships at the shrine of Horatio Alger. But let him get any kind of decent Trendex, and he automatically has to protect himself against the kill."

"That's a pretty cynical set of observations for a girl who bakes Girl Scout cookies. Do you honestly believe it's true, or is it something you read in The Video Almanac?"

"Maybe you're right," she laughed. "Yes, you probably are. I tend to talk most violently about things I understand least." She was craning her neck now. "I did come in with a young man tonight, didn't I? And I very likely sent him into the direct line of fire—namely the bar. Will you excuse me, Mr. Creighton? I'd better go and make like *Little Women*."

Jim watched her go, swinging that lovely rump ever so slightly and unconsciously, and noticed, as two guests separated for a second, that Lee Gardiner had discovered a way to jump off the wagon in something like record breaking time. He was pouring one drink down his throat and extending another glass to the bartender nearest him for a refill.

Wally Brunow was the man to seek out, and Jim found him, leaning on the piano and singing along with a good Rodgers and Hart medley.

"I just found an inch of free space in this bargain basement, Wally," he notified. "Hurry up before they fill it."

"Anything for you, pard," Wally confided, padding along with him for a few yards. "You're such a good old friend I'll even take Ginny off your hands and bed her down for the night. Nothin's too good for my friends."

"Fill me in on Ginny Grant, Wally," Jim said, taking another glance at her at the long bar; Gardiner was downing a drink as if Prohibition were just about to go into effect, and she was evidently doing her unshowy best to talk him out of it. "Bucky and I are paying her salary, but Evelyn hired her. I don't know anything at all about her. Apparently you do."

"What's the question category, Jim? Business or pleasure?" Wally inquired, nudging him.

"Frankly, I don't know yet. It depends on what facts and figures you come up with for me."

"Oh, I get it. Fran hopped off to Cabott Island."

"Now how in the hell did you know that? I haven't said boo to you in close to three months."

"I'm unlike you, pard," Wally rejoined. "I read the papers. Ed Sullivan printed it, today or yesterday. What're you, too cheap to get yourself a clipping service?"

"First thing in the morning. Now tell me. How did she fall into my lap? Who is she?"

Wally recognized that the question begged for a thoughtful answer, and took a breath before he plunged.

"Then you've been out of touch, Jim," he began. "You haven't been with us for lunch at Toots's and The Holland House and Bleeck's where she's been the main topic of conversation."

"Who's us?"

"Us. We. Guys from NBC, Columbia, RBS, Dumont. Everyone who's droolingly watched her move that mean *tokas* down the research department corridors. Everybody exhumed the old Mae West and Monroe gags about her because she seemed to be asking for it. A few guys you and I know dated her—Al Gallagher, Morry Spector, Eddie Moran. They say they made it with her, but you know them. They made it with every chick in town except Ethel Barrymore, and they promise you she'll be sayin' yes by Tuesday."

"What do you think? Did any of them make it with her?" Jim asked. He remembered that Gallagher, Spector and Moran weren't just network employees. They were executives; men whose word could have accommodating, ambitious girls owning huge blocks of Manhattan Island overnight.

"Who the hell knows?" Wally shrugged. The pianist had disposed of Rodgers and Hart and was going virtuoso with the more involved works of Harold Arlen. "Nobody pays any attention to talk of a fast roll in the hay, either for sure or dreamed up. One rumor seems to hold water, though—that she was Finnegan's tootsie-pie for a while at Monarch."

Last year, when he had been the unquestioned head of Monarch Broadcasting, Asa L. Finnegan had gone into his office, taken a pistol from his desk drawer, and blown his brains out.

"Finnegan?" Jim frowned. "Really?"

"That's the scoop."

The acre of living room was becoming, if possible, even more crowded as more and more guests streamed in. The pianist was making a one-man symphony of *That Old Black Magic*, and another one of the assembled applicant prostitutes was making a trojan effort in the limited space to dance to it and keep drinking at the same time.

Everyone seemed to be drinking more and talking more frenziedly. Bruce Cavanaugh, Redmond's bland-looking hatchet, was forgetting his private eye duties by getting conspicuously loaded. Glasses somehow tinkled more loudly, laughs rippled more piercingly from odd compartments of the room, and voices became more enthusiastic. Lee Gardiner was still at the bar, busying himself in talk with the agency camp follower as he held a glass in a zigzaggy way that announced it had been quite heavy to lift.

Ginny Grant was missing. Soon the patrol of Jim's eyes located her. She was sitting on a low hassock, being receptively animated in conversation with Eric Miller, one of Ira Frazier's crackerjack ad men. Men were looking at her, at the way she screwed a cigarette into her bright red holder, at the way she cocked her head a bit too luxuriously as she let Miller flick his lighter to it, as she sat back and took in a lot of smoke, relishing it for a moment before she released it from her sensuous mouth, as she laughed fully at Miller's timid little jokes, as she seemed to be presumably available for everything and anything a man wanted of her.

"What about her dead husband?" Jim asked. "She told me she's a widow."

"Can't help you there," Wally said, taking two drinks from a passing tray and handing one to Jim. "Or with much of anything else about her background. Go and check her application at the RBS files. Maybe that'll help."

"One more question," Jim persisted. "If she has all she has, what's she doing working for me for sixty-five a week?"

"That's another good question. And I'm telling you: I know from nothing when it comes to the essentials. All I know is that she appears to be the sort of young dame we read about in all the Tillie and Mac books when we were kids, the kind who spells trouble. You know: T-R-U-B-B-L-E. Let me go now, pard. There's some qualified poon over yonder named Jody I used to know who mixed memory with desire when I was a boy genius. She's an upper-bracket hooker, now, so I'd better tread lightly. Good luck, pard."

Within the next half hour Lee Gardiner gave every proclamation of being entirely on his own. At least twice he happily accosted Jim, on his sea-going staggers about the spacious room, and confided, "I was on the bright blue wagon for too, too long. Z'about time I tipped my ol' hat to John Barleycorn a little, right?" The guests had increased in number, but a subtle quiet had substantially begun to settle over the party. At one point, Jim noted, Monica Enders cursed at the man nearest her and insisted, "Find some way to get rid of him before he creates a scene!"

Jim had just accepted his fifth drink from one of the bartenders when he saw Gardiner being quietly ejected from the party. Ginny was knee-deep in mercurial conversation with

Eric Miller again. She gave chaste signals that she couldn't be less interested.

This would have been her one chance, Jim decided. She could have gone after Gardiner. But she didn't. Instead she waited the cautious number of minutes and then found Jim.

"Do you remember what I said before about baking Girl Scout cookies?" she asked in that bottled-in-cream voice.

"Yes. I remember."

"I hereby resign."

"Oh?"

"I get paralyzed when someone gets noticeably drunk, even someone who's brought me. I live at one-oh-one Cornelia, second floor front. I'm leaving in another minute, by myself. Distinctly and without fanfare by myself. If you're interested, I'll be there in one hour from now. The nameplate in the vestibule reads *Grant*. The door will be open. If you're interested."

Jim nodded. "I'm interested."

"Good night."

He observed the extremely clever way she disappeared from the party. He got into a busy talk with Monica Enders, who dropped all kinds of suave hints that she would be willing to have him help put out the lights later. He chatted for a minute with Bucky who made a raspy exit with Mrs. Stander. He kept drinking as he moved from known guest to known guest. He said what he imagined he was supposed to say, and forty minutes later was in a taxi.

"Cornelia Street," he directed.

Then he was pressing the nameplate button that read *Grant*. He heard the hoarse bell that released the door, and he was mounting the rickety stairs. He decided he had had a trifle too much to drink, but it wouldn't pose any great problem.

The door was open.

"Hello, Mr. Creighton," she said.

She was wearing the most exquisitely skin-smooth night-gown he had ever seen.

It was transparent.

"I think you'd better close the door," she said.

CHAPTER SEVEN

H IS BREATH WAS a sharp pain in his lungs as he extended his arms and she invaded them, whispering huskily, "Oh, love me, darling …"

Beneath the dignity of high cheek bones her full lips were parted in red wonder, trusting, demanding. He bent to cover them with an urgency that seemed to startle them both. From moment to moment as they kissed, he drew back, losing himself behind the screen of night that darkened the fantastic beauty of surrender in her eyes.

"Oh, please, please, oh my dearest, love me love me love me now …" she was pleading, and they were drifting over great chasms of space and then they suddenly were out of the cavernous living room and in a tiny, intimate, warm bedroom. There was a faint night light above the neat, virginal looking single bed. The spread was pulled back in deliberate seduction.

Greedily his fingers removed the gown and a hushed cry of delight broke from his throat. Hers was a vibrantly alive body, supple and yielding, molded in invitation. There was the maze of zippers and buttons and then they were together, kissing fiercely, clutching in hunger and need. She was ravenous and wildly responsive.

For a long time afterwards—there was no way of gauging time—they breathed heavily, still touching one another, still reaching out for fleeting nibbles of kisses. There was, most of all, the towering joy of realizing that neither was embarrassed by the light, that the love they had shared together—and it had been love, certainly love—had meaning, dimension, depth, full reality. Beside him, being cradled by him, she was more lovely than before, and it was impossible to imagine having ever been without her. Or of ever being without her again.

A portable radio on her bedroom bureau was playing *Diamonds For Her Furs*, softly, caressingly, when the telephone next to her bed rang. Its jangle was remotely familiar and he recalled dimly that it had rung seven or eight times when they'd first come into this room.

"Damn," she muttered with no particular annoyance, and leaned across his chest to pick up the receiver. "Do you have twenty million dollars to bet me that this isn't going to be Lee?"

"Hello? ... Yes, Lee," she said, and impishly twisted around to grin an I-told-you-so grin at Jim. Her perfume, the same perfume that had plagued him since yesterday (*had he first seen her only yesterday?*) roused desire again, and he felt majestically ten feet tall again.

"Lee, dearest, I know ... Yes, I know you tried your best. But it just didn't take this time ... No, Lee, tonight is out. I can't see you.... No, I've been asleep for hours and hours, and I love you, but I simply can't cook bacon and eggs for you now. Perhaps another time, all right? ... Yes, Lee, I understand ... Lee ... Lee, dear, yes, I know, but I have to hang up now.... Lee, I know about your book and how hard you tried ... Lee, please don't make me a horror and make me hang up on you. Will you be a nice boy and say good night and let me go back to sleep? And we'll talk again tomorrow or sometime, if you like? ... Thank you, darling. You get home and turn in and I *promise* I'll phone you and see how you are. I promise. Good night, dear."

She replaced the receiver, and silently nestled against Jim's bare chest for a moment. "I'm sorry," she asserted. "That was on the verge of getting a little sticky. Wouldn't you know it would come at the least propitious time?"

"Did he fall very hard off the wagon?" Jim asked, carefully avoiding the real question, the one that wanted to know if she had ever given herself to Gardiner as she had given herself to Jim Creighton.

"It was about par, I guess," Ginny answered, bringing the covers up to their chins as she squeezed his arm and impetuously kissed his shoulder. "Lee is a complete anomaly. For some perverse reason he struggles to give the impression of being the proud son from Idiot Corners, but actually he's a divine writer."

"Yes, I've heard that."

"And lost. That's old hat these days, isn't it? Saying a talented writer is lost, like right out of Scott Fitzgerald. But he is. I called him dear and darling because I meant to. I've read his book at least a half dozen times and I feel like Ginny-the-Mother-Hen toward him."

"Earlier today you told me he was your fiance."

"Did I? Truly? Well, maybe I meant that, too, if you're flexible with the word. I've known Lee for a year, maybe a bit longer, and when I need to be taken somewhere if I don't have a date, or if I'm alone and I need someone to play a game of stud poker with me, Lee always is available. I give parties here once every three and a half thousand years, and he's always available, to, you know, pitch in and lend a little amoral support."

Jim nodded, wishing he could rid himself of the feelings of screwball jealousy, a jealousy he knew he didn't genuinely feel. "Lee, the available onion peeler," he said.

"Well, yes, but that's a more brutal way of putting it. And will you kindly tell me why we're talking about Lee?" she laughed, moving her hand possessively over his shoulders. "We could be discussing more immediate points of interest, you know. Such as

Algeria, and whether Debbie and Eddie will spend their fiftieth birthdays together, after all."

"Yes. We could."

"Hold tight," Ginny said. "I'll get us some cigarettes." She hoisted herself gently out of the bed and started for the other room. He was conscious again of the flawless curves of her body, of the instinctively sexual way she moved. The ripe perfume was still a major part of the air.

Jim leaned back, half listening to Sinatra come in on a second chorus of *The Lady Is A Tramp*, and let his thoughts crowd with the stifling images of what the consequences might be of his being here. He was a Wheel who had never asked to be a Wheel, had never sincerely raced after becoming a Wheel. Colter Small from high school had discreetly warned him against becoming something he wasn't destined to be. Evelyn Shoreham had told him the same thing, and in more vehement words, only a few hours ago. And he knew it, himself. He was wearing a false face. A laugh-cry theatrical mask that was a vulgarity because it could be turned upside down so often with such deceptive ease. He belonged back in Haylesburg, Pennsylvania, selling men's hose and acting the simpering husband of the fire-chief's daughter, going along with the Elks Club crowd as they sniggeringly planned their annual Stunt Night.

And here he was, bucking for sophistication, a realm which displeased and continually threatened him. Ginny was the only thing to come into his tattered life that added up to a promise of possible peace. And even so, he would have to be on his constant guard, to make sure that the glistening hayseed wouldn't show too perceptibly.

She was back now with cigarettes, gingerly placing a lighted one between his lips, and he was acutely conscious of the fullness of her marvelous breasts. "You look positively beautiful, lying there," she said and met his arms again. "Tired, maybe?"

"Exhausted. Ruthlessly exhausted."

"Good!" she announced. "I'm glad."

"Glad I'm exhausted? And you the angel of network mercy?"

"No, I'm glad you said exhausted, and not spent. Men do say they're spent, don't they? I hate it. Spent is an evil, weasle word. Oh, I'm so glad you came!"

"Yes?"

"Yes. And it's all supposed to be so shameful, isn't it? This assignation stuff, right out of old Erich Von Stroheim movies. It never entered my mind when I applied for a job at Rockland that something like this was bound to happen. I'm almost waiting for a crack of thunder to strike from an old Warner Brothers picture right now. Will it happen? I've always been terrified of thunder."

"Ginny …"

"You say it so wonderfully. I've wanted to hear you say 'Ginny' in just that way for such a long time," she laughed. "You may as well know all the sleazy facts now. I've watched you on my ancient ten-inch TV since you began your show. I've wanted to hear the way you'd call me 'Ginny'."

"You seem so … unsurprised by everything."

"What's everything?" she inquired. "Your being here?" He nodded. "I probably will be, after you've left. I'll be confused and as guilty as anything once you've gone home. But now I'm just happy, purring like a cat because you're holding me. I very likely won't have the nerve to look you in the eye on Monday morning, if I'm still working for you."

"If? Why wouldn't you be?"

"I don't know. We didn't talk ourselves into this tonight. We played little eye games this morning in the elevator and here and there during the conference, but none of this was actually, consciously planned, was it? Not by me, anyway, not that consciously. I don't deny that I'm sort of batty in the belfry, in an innocuous way, but I'm direct and I never lie. I simply wanted you to come here and make love to me. No mysterious, lurking motivations. I don't know what's going on in your head. That's why I say I may be fired on Monday morning."

"You don't sound terribly worried about it."

"That's what I've been trying to tell you," Ginny said, moving her head an inch or so on his chest and tracing her finger down a vein on his hand. "I have a boomerang personality. I might blow up into a million pieces when you go home and wonder just what the heck drove me to inviting you up here, when I need to hold onto this job so badly. I've acted like a dewy-eyed kid just out of secretarial school who's both impetuous and—promiscuous. And basically I don't think I'm either." The green shell ash tray fell off the bed as she moved again, and she nervously retrieved it from the floor. "I do prattle on, don't I?"

Jim recalled Wally Brunow, and Wally's talk about Spector, Gallagher and Moran. And Finnegan. Somehow it didn't fit. Nothing was easier than to say that a pretty, sensual-looking girl slept around, particularly if she worked in a setting owned and operated by men. He had no outsized illusions about Ginny Grant; surely she'd been around in this network jungle. But certainly it was much too melodramatic to imagine that she had invited him here for the frosty purpose of advancing a career. That off-color joke had gone out with the swallowing of goldfish, hadn't it?

"You prattle, Ginny," he answered, touching her hair. "And you're very lovely."

Meaningfully she turned to meet his gaze, silently and effectively. Her hand raised to clutch the back of his head. She murmured a pleading jumble of words he felt rather than heard, and hungrily offered her lips. From the radio, a sound of gutsy, blue trumpet combed the air of the low-ceiling room.

"Roy was very dear and I loved him as deeply as it's possible to love a man," Ginny said about her husband later, as Jim sat on her living room couch. She built him a Scotch and water in the opened kitchen as she talked, and went back to pour a glass of milk for herself. His drink was strong.

"Do you want to hear all this?" she asked, returning, sitting in the chair nearest him. "It's like looking at photographs of Baby and Aunt Maude; it never really interests anyone except the immediate family." She had wrapped herself in a tailored satin housecoat and she was bare of makeup. Jim had dressed, except for his tie. He discovered, as he took his first sip (she had told him there was a full bottle of Vat 69 *on* the kitchen counter and he could help himself as he pleased), that he couldn't remember when he'd been more relaxed than he was now.

"I want to hear it, Ginny," he said. He liked the inauspicious, almost stark simplicity of her small apartment. The solid colored furniture looked as if it had been chosen by a woman and designed for a man. There were odd lamps and odder knick-knacks, and the sloping quality of the floor and even the walls proclaimed that it was part of a tottering old downtown apartment that would disintegrate by the end of the month. The far wall was covered by a series of bookshelves which contained, he had noticed, books, pamphlets and record albums which obviously had been gone through, again and again.

Now she was on the floor, her head on his knee, gently massaging his ankle as she sipped her milk. "We were married less than a week after he was discharged from that awful Korea thing, right here in New York. I remember that those offices down around Foley Square, or wherever it is, wouldn't open till nine or some such forlorn hour to sell you a marriage license, and we spent something like three hours walking around downtown New York, hand in hand, playing funny word games and talking about how we'd grown up. He was from here in Queens, and I was from Savannah."

"Savannah? Georgia?"

"Mmm."

"You sound about as Southern as Grace Kelly."

She nodded and chuckled. "I know. Isn't it disgraceful? I was considered the throwback in the Clay family. Everyone around me talked in dialects that were right out of mushmelon and Rhett Butler and Hattie McDaniel, and I arose sounding as Northern as a Yankee can possibly get. I didn't work at it, I don't think, but there it was. So. We'd met at Barnard. Or, at any rate, I was going to Barnard College, studying journalism of all things, and he was at Columbia, majoring in law. He was built along your lines—a long drink of water and almost cadaverously thin and with an Adam's Apple that couldn't have been more prominent—and he orated like nobody's business. I had this merciless crush on him and all I was attempting to do was to get him to kiss me, and all he was interested in doing was to orate about the jury system and against capital punishment, in the most conspicuous ways. And the more juvenile he sounded, the more he sounded like Clarence Darrow."

"Did he become a lawyer?"

"No. That was the funny part, the unfair part," Ginny said, stiffening a bit. "He went through every conceivable hell in Korea. He was the bad-luck kid who got sent into every bloody battle they turned up with. He saw most of his friends cut down, and he somehow managed to walk through it all without a scratch. It went on for two years without a letup. He survived and he came back. We were married and we spent our honeymoon in Asbury

Park, of all onbeat places. And exactly one week after we *got* back to New York, just seven days afterwards, he crossed the street when the light said green, and some drunken truck driver for one of those rotten moving van companies thought he saw a green light and killed Roy. Broad daylight. As undramatic as broad daylight."

"I'm sorry."

"They found him and arrested him. He'd been warned once before about drinking on the job, and he'd sworn to behave himself because he had all these kids at home. They found out he'd been drinking his second fifth of gin for the day. There was a lot of yammering back and forth, and finally they let him go. And Roy was dead. Can I fix you another drink?"

"Okay," said Jim, noting with some surprise that his glass was empty. "Thanks."

There was more of it, a great deal more of it. It began with Roy, ended with Roy, and the spaces were filled in with the wonderfully scatterbrained news of her grandmother's tatting and her uncle in Savannah who had written four books which hadn't been published but which had striven to prove that the South had won the Civil War.

"You have a remarkable talent," she said. "You can drink and keep drinking and never get drunk. I watched you through that forgettable party tonight. You stayed at it, and here at my place I've poured out not only my heart but most of my bottle of Scotch, and you're as clear-eyed as my sister Eloise's infant boy. How did you perfect it?"

"Don't be so awed," Jim laughed as he downed his drink and wondered if he could feel free enough in her home to ask for another. "I'm the quietly simpering gent who turns up at parties and stands at the dark walls like a wallflower with one julep, and who invariably ends up on Skid Row. Please don't get me going on that."

"Nonsense. You're all man. Every move you make is masculine," Ginny declared, rising to her feet and switching off the ghostly overhead light before she returned to join him. "Pardon me for going all Southern all of a sudden, but the prime requisite for a man is that he knows how to hold his likkah. And you know how to do that."

"Ginny," Jim said. "Come here."

"Yes, my dearest."

He lowered her to his lap and kissed her again as his hand moved with sudden freeness over her quivering body. "You are a very special person," he said solemnly. "I think you are very special."

"Are you feeling your likkah, suh?"

"No, I'm feeling my Ginny, ma'am."

"Fresh!"

"Yeah," he nodded happily. "I'll see you again, won't I? Soon?"

Ginny's short fingernails dug into his scalp. "I hope so," she whispered, more seriously than he had expected. "I hope so. So very much."

He accepted another drink and knew that it was time to leave, that the grimmest times of his life had been ones in which he had overstayed his welcome.

"We'll talk tomorrow," Jim promised.

"Let's do better than that," Ginny said. "I'll call you. First thing in the morning."

"Good."

"Provided you leave me your unlisted number."

"Double good. Remember this," he smiled and rattled off his new number. "You remember it?"

"Take one more good look at my thigh. It's branded there. Noon?"

"Noon."

"Then go," Ginny said as she slid off his lap and moved away from him. "Knot that tie with some semblance of accuracy and find a taxi downstairs. I'm desperately sleepy."

"—Well ...?"

"And I make another old fashioned point of sleeping alone. Don't blame me. Blame the fusty traditions of Savannah. I'll call you, dearest."

"Noon," Jim repeated, getting up.

"On the button. Thank you so much for not struggling with me. I appreciate it."

"Noon," Jim said as he kissed her again and headed for the door. "Good night, Ginny."

"Thank you again," Ginny reminded.

"For what?"

"For you. For kissing me. For holding me. For being so tender. For listening so long to me without a yawn and for loving me."

He wobbled down the steps to the vestibule and the street that led to a cab. He found one after an interminable amount of time, and mumbled his address. He got home and remembered to take off his clothes before he dropped into bed.

"Ginny," he said aloud. "Noon. Please call me."

CHAPTER EIGHT

SHE DIDN'T PHONE.

At half past eleven he was wakened by a call from Evelyn Shoreham. He told her he'd just risen and would get back to her a little later. Less than a minute later Bucky called, and he told him the same thing. He was attempting to rinse the flannel out of his mouth five minutes after that when his brother Harry telephoned and invited him to lunch; he advised Harry an important call was expected and would he ring back in about a half hour?

Then there was an obstinate fearsome silence in the high-ceilinged apartment.

He padded to the kitchen in the Finchley silk robe one of his happy TV guests had sent him a few months ago, and splattered some water into a pot for instant coffee. The fact that Mrs. Wentsmann wasn't around vacantly pleased him. Scissoring his long fingers through his close-cropped hair, *but it still needs cutting, doesn't it?* he reminded himself; *hope I remember to hustle over to The Algonquin this afternoon for a quickie trim*, he walked from room to room in search of a cigarette and then discovered two unopened packs in the pocket of his robe. He wondered if he'd actually jotted down Ginny's phone number or if he'd imagined he had.

A quarter of twelve. She'd assured him once or twice that she wasn't an impetuous girl, that she never did anything on impulse. But the walls would hardly come tumbling down, she must have known, if she decided to phone a few minutes earlier than noon. Look out, buddy, he advised himself; it's bad when life starts getting like the Nineteenth Century songs and every minute seems like an hour. Believe that and you'll soon be picking petals off daisies. Lord, let's hope you didn't transmit any anxiety when you left her last night. Or this morning. What time was it? When did you finally decide to go cavalier and recognize that she must've been beat?

The powdered coffee helped a lot, and he realized gradually that the faint banging at the head and the distant jumps in his stomach meant that he had something akin to a hangover. He'd been hung before, certainly—and often to the point where he'd wondered if hangovers could cause immediate death and, if not, why not. But since he'd begun on the RBS treadmill five months ago, except for an occasionally overdramatic grouch and the morning's desperate need for just an hour's more sleep, he'd been able to fight off all alcoholic wounds with no more than a few minutes of spartan battle.

He grinned wryly now as he downed the coffee and puttered through the maze of cupboards for a loaf of bread. A king-sized but not too painful hangover was to be welcomed into the house now and then. He couldn't swiftly remember everything that had happened to him last night, but he did recollect all the grog he'd put away over the period of a few hours. How would it be described by Pierre Mendez-France, the great statesman and milk drinker he'd interviewed by phonetape back in March or early April? *"Formidable!"* A great people, the French. They could comment on every and any complexity of life by giving it the simple tag, *"Formidable!"* No excess was too excess to earn such a magnificent description.

When the telephone rang at exactly three minutes before noon, Jim rushed to it in the bedroom, carrying his empty coffee cup. She got the message, he thought jubilantly, and lifted the pink receiver before it sounded a second time.

"Hello," he said, feeling frivolous and sophisticatedly sixteen-years-old, feeling like tattersall vests and ornate white piping, feeling like the toothy impersonators in ninth-rate night clubs who announce they're going to do Cary Grant and then clench their teeth and exclaim, "Ju-deeee! You'ah one grand hunk of gel, Ju-deeeee!"

"Jim?"

"You're a few minutes early," he said. "What happened?"

"A few minutes ... Jim, did you expect me to call you?"

He tightened and sat upright. The voice belonged to Fran.

"Fran, hello. I thought you were ... someone from the office. I can hear Honolulu and Kenya without any trouble, but there's usually no such thing as a clear connection with Cabott Island.

"No wonder, today. You've heard about everything, haven't you?"

Impatiently, Jim fished for another cigarette. "Heard about what, Fran?" he asked guardedly.

"The storm," said Fran. "It began at ten last night and went on through most of the night. Do you mean you don't know anything about it?"

"Storm? I went to Monica Enders' thing a little after the show and didn't go near a radio. Are you all right? Fran ... is anything wrong?"

"Oh, no, I'm all right, and the Fraziers are fine, too," she said, giving that painstakingly appeasing laugh to let him know that there's never any real reason for worry. "But all of it's been on the radio and television, I'm sure. We had a ninetymile gale that tore the roofs off a dozen houses less than a mile away from here. You know Mildred and Bob Jailer. Their bungalow was completely turned over, but they're all right. Jim, it couldn't have been more frightening. We had it here at about midnight and it kept blowing for what seemed like forever, but there wasn't any damage at all, thank Heaven."

"I don't like the way you sound," Jim said apprehensively. "I'll get right out there. Are there boats running?"

"Oh, Jim …" Fran tried to placate.

"Things must be getting back to shape. The lines couldn't be down or you wouldn't have been able to call me. But you sound strange. Still frightened?"

"No, Jim. Honestly. Now that's exactly what I didn't mean to do: scare you. I'm perfectly all right. We had some exciting moments here for a while but no one was hurt. Ira will tell you." Fran was speaking rapidly now. "If I'd thought I might upset you, with all that's on your mind I wouldn't have called you. Please forget it, Jim. Truly. Look, here's Ira trying to tell …"

Then Ira Frazier was giving out with his booming Santa Claus laugh and assuring Jim that there had been all perdition to pay for a time last night, but everything was clear as crystal now. "Little surprised you didn't catch it on the radio, old sport," Ira added, a touch more sober and confidential than before. "Frances just chased back to the porch with Madge, so I can talk. Any time I think of you, I think of you reading the AP tickers on the latest developments in Siberia or Port Jervis. Or at least keeping an ear to the radio. Oughta stop, I guess."

"Ira, I give you my word," Jim insisted and was astonished with the onslaught of guilt which he suspected was scarcely necessary. "I would've found a way to get up there in a minute if I'd known what was going on. This call is the first I've had an inkling of …"

"Sure," Ira chuckled. "Sorry I said anything. We're all shipshape. Sorry I made Frances call."

"What do you mean, you made Frances call? What's it all about?"

"She didn't want to, you know. Didn't want to trouble you, was the way she put it. I got her to do it, Madge and I. Seems to me, Jim, you two're sort of drifting apart, as if Frances wants to always do the right thing by you, but you're never really around. Maybe it's not my business, but I thought being a friend ..."

"Let me talk with Fran again," Jim directed, angry and helpless.

"That's not necessary, Jim. I have a word or two more I want to ..."

"Let me talk with Fran. Right now."

Fran was back on the line after a prolonged few minutes and Jim's grip on the telephone was rigid. "I gather you've been hanging out the family-wash for the Fraziers, Fran," he said sharply. "If you feel there's a strain between us, the Fraziers aren't the ones to confide in; they're not close friends and they can't tell you anything you don't know. If you have anything to say about our marriage, why can't you say it to me?"

"Please, Jim. I didn't say anything, I swear. Ira got after me last night right here in the living room, even before the storm started. He began to say I wasn't happy and he tried to put words in my mouth. Honestly, Jim. I'd never say anything about ... anything to anyone except you. Please believe that. I didn't even want to call you now and bother you ..."

"*Are* you unhappy, Fran?"

"Oh, no, Jim! What a silly thing to say."

"Would you rather come on back home?" he asked, hoping the question sounded neither encouraging nor waspish.

"... I want to do what's right. I know you're so busy and I'm only in the way till the pressure lets up on Labor Day."

The speech was memorized and spoken with pathetically measured cadence, and he discovered his throat was becoming dry. He had never told her he loved her, not even on the night he had made her pregnant, and he wondered why the word *love* had been so difficult to say. Or why any important words of endearment or even hate, had never come spontaneously. He neither wanted her home with him now nor away from him. He could find no way to tell her what he felt. There was no way to tell himself.

"Forgive me, Fran," he said. "I didn't mean to bark at you. I know what a nosey old lady Ira is; I should've known he'd be getting on your neck the second you got up there."

"Both of them have been awfully nice to me," Fran defended. "Last night when the storm acted like it was getting a little too close for comfort, Ira couldn't have been more concerned about me. He was just like a father."

"I'll phone you tomorrow night," Jim promised suddenly, eager to be free not because of Ginny Grant but because the sensation of helplessness with her was so damning. As usual, Fran offered no argument, not even a veiled questioning. They talked for another few seconds and he watched his damp hand tremulously replace the receiver.

To keep himself busy, he toasted a slice of bread, which he didn't eat, and boiled some more water for coffee, which became cold before he remembered to take his third sip. The telephone was silent. He walked through the apartment, opening windows on this wretchedly hot day *(I planned to see about having that air conditioner fixed; why did it slip my mind? can you reach them on Saturdays?)* and inevitably noted the phone. Maybe it was temporarily out of order. He lifted the receiver, listened to the soft, lulling hum, and placed it back on its cradle.

She hadn't promised to call him just in order to get him to leave.

Where was she?

Only warm air came in through the windows and, although the early afternoon appeared to be bright, the expensive apartment was unnaturally dark. No reason to switch on lights, which would have given him something to do, he thought, but weren't you entitled to some natural light when you were paying so damn much money? He passed through the foyer and blinked at his rumpled jacket on a chair. In the inside breast pocket he found the envelope. Her telephone number was scribbled on it.

Hopefully he took it to the breakfast nook wall phone and wondered what would happen if he were to go through with it. It wasn't quite half-past twelve. She'd dialed him at noon but the line had been busy, and she'd rushed out for a carton of milk. Or she'd overslept. Or her clock had stopped. Or something. Maybe the tender tease. *Yes, I said I'd call, but I'm an old-fashioned Jawjuh girl. We wear crinoline and fix juleps for our men folks and we never make calls.*

Jim was so absorbed in the galaxy of possibilities that he wasn't wholly conscious of the ring when it did sound. He darted for the receiver, desperate to hear her voice. "Hello?"

"Hi. It's Harry again," his brother said.

"Oh … uh, hello."

"What about that lunch? I'll be closing up the shop in another ten, fifteen minutes and I can be at Costello's by one or a little after. I want to start for the shore before it gets too late."

They had been promising to have this lunch for the past week—Harry's wife Martha and their five kids were away for the summer, too—and Jim knew he couldn't goof out without a legitimate explanation. "Harry, that call I was waiting for still hasn't come. Look, you're about an eighty-cent cab ride away from here.

Why don't you taxi over and I'll whip us up some drinks? The closets're full of fancy-pantsy cans of food nobody around here touches. You mind?"

"Fair enough. I'll see you later."

That, of course, hadn't been smart, either, he decided. He still owed calls to Evelyn and Bucky and he didn't want to waste the waiting time to ring them. Somebody—had it been Bucky—had advised him that one private telephone number wasn't enough, that he should have at least three, but he'd balked at the idea. The five separate lines in his office were more than enough, he'd answered; his home was not to be a surrogate office and, anyway, he was hardly in his home at all any more.

Getting last night's battered clothes out of the way, Jim tentatively came to the decision to get rid of the phone number, too. If she phoned, fine. If she didn't, he'd figure some way to deal with her later. But he was a grown man, not a gluey-eyed kid suffering his first violent crush, and this heavy-panting stuff was geared for Harry's boy, who was about to reach his teens.

He tuned the radio in to WRBS for possible news on last night's Cabott Island storm, heard only a taped interview with one of next year's former movie stars, and went about patching up the front part of the apartment. *Maybe she'll call*, he thought. *There's no reason why she shouldn't. Something happened, something like crossed lines or too many busy signals or running out for that quart of milk. She may be something like what Wally Brunow suggested, but she's not a fly-by-night. I was the one she kissed last night, and it had genuine meaning for her.*

The WRBS news flashes came in during the first sixteen bars of an Ella Fitzgerald solo, much as expected. It had been Flanders Bryce Redmond's brilliant idea that newscasts, even the ordinary local ones, ought to be pitched in without warning on radio over weekends, to give the listener the extra sensation of being there.

Terry Lawrence, one of the best of Fat Red's young announcing brood, breathlessly announced last night's semi-holocaust on Cabott. The report was fast yet complete. There had been a lot of money damage, but only two people had been injured. One of those accidents of nature. You get scared, even though you know at one astonishing point that you're going to come out of it alive and not too shaken.

There was a fleeting shock in recalling again that Fran had actually been in danger last night, but the urge to rush to her was almost glibly easy to erase. The marriage had never been a happy one. He had never over-extended himself to her, probably, but then Fran had never really given him any reason to. Now he took out some ice for Harry's visit, and tried to figure why, after eight years with her, he hadn't been able to either go or stay.

He had made her pregnant on that Christmas Eve eight years ago, just a few hours after he'd met her near the pastrami sandwich counter at one of those abysmal publishers' parties on the East Side. She couldn't have been more acquiescent; he couldn't have been more staid in his drunkenness; and when he'd awkwardly asked her afterwards if she'd been fully prepared for him, she had merely hugged him and announced that she adored him. It had taken fewer than two months, and a terrified visit to a doctor, to verify his fear and make it plain that she hadn't understood his question.

"We'll have to do something," he had told her shakily, summoning up the dreadful image of the alley-way office, the nurse with the bad skin, and the doctor with the dirty fingernails who performed his operations on hard kitchen tables.

"Yes, Jim" Fran had said, with the instantaneous hope and trust that made him aware she again had misunderstood what he was saying.

"I mean … a doctor. I can ask someone I know and come up with a doctor who knows what he's …"

The saucer eyes and the indignation. "But that's murder!"

He could have made a getaway then, of course, and nothing serious would have happened to him. She was from Salt Lake, a kind of dedicated typist with no family and seemingly no friends in New York. There wasn't the glimmer of feeling for her; he'd begun talking with her at that party largely because there hadn't been anyone else of interest to talk with, and he'd taken her back to her gloomy apartment on the West Side and stayed the night with her for no reason that he would ever be able to determine except that he had been intolerably lonely on that Christmas Eve and his own career had been struggling for life on a treadmill that kept breaking down.

It didn't cross her logically simple mind that anything could happen other than a quick wedding. He had been dating an excruciating desirable girl from White Plains, a girl he'd hoped to marry and who wouldn't have refused him, a girl who, by one of those rotten strokes of luck that had plagued him through his life, had meant to join him on Christmas Eve but who at the last minute had flown to Florida with her parents for the holidays.

He made no promises to Frances Gerrick, the uncomplicated Utah girl who delighted in confession magazines and believed that the actors on the screen made up the dialogue as they went along. For a while he stayed away from her. She knew where he lived and where he worked, but she made no attempt to contact him. For more than a week, shuttling between relief and the sweats, he imagined that a little time and a few magic words could blank out that Christmas Eve, and that the weeks that followed could perhaps even make it all a transient nightmare that hadn't actually occurred.

He confided in no one. He immersed himself in his monotonous job at the WRBS news-desk and on two more occasions met Leslie, the girl from White Plains, without letting her suspect for a moment that anything troubled him. On the other long nights which yawned before him after the news copy had been cleaned up, he trudged home to his suddenly bleak one-and-a-half rooms on Bleecker Street, where he paced feverishly, defended and argued with himself, and finally went to sleep with the help of a pint of bourbon.

At four o'clock in the afternoon, on January 30th, he phoned her at her office and told her to meet him in twenty minutes at the Mayflower Coffee Shop at 51st. She explained that she couldn't get out until five, but she'd meet him at ten after five. When she arrived, her eyes still trusting, still hopeful, he recalled that he hadn't been able to dredge up a picture of her in his mind from the last time they'd been together. She was wearing that lumpishly bulky but practical beaver coat, a small beret that wasn't practical, and she was prettier than he had recollected. She was carrying a spanking new copy of *Modern Screen*.

They spent a very long time over coffee in one of the prim booths as the shop became more crowded, and the waitress glared at them each time she passed their table. Over the past week Jim had prepared and memorized a speech he was certain would have impressed a trial judge. But now he remembered none of it. He told her he would marry her as soon as they got their blood test.

Fran squeezed his hand, fought tears that wouldn't be contained, and thanked him. He lighted a second cigarette with the ash of a first one, and wondered why he'd chosen this place to meet her. They sold no liquor and he was desperately in need of a drink.

The telephone still hadn't rung by the time Harry appeared, and Jim glumly stuck the phone number into his slacks pocket. They shook hands, a habit they'd started years ago, although there seldom was a week in which they didn't see one another.

"Am I seeing things or are you putting on a belly?" Jim asked warmly, ushering him into the front room, keenly glad to see him. "Another couple of months and you won't be able to button that jacket."

"Blame it on Martha's potato latkes," Harry grinned, rolling the inevitable butt of a stogie leisurely around in his mouth. "She got on this heavy starch diet for me before she took the kids to the shore, and I haven't been the same since. By the way, she was sorry she didn't get to see you before they all took off. Little Jim, especially, He's perfected a moon rocket he wanted you to put your okay on."

"Well, why didn't somebody tell me?" he complained. "I'm always available for that big guy. What the hell are we all, strangers or something? Why can't we get together more often?"

At the portable bar, Jim built a Scotch and soda for Harry, and decided that a shorty for himself wouldn't hurt. The love he felt for his kid brother (*it always sounds crazy to call him that; he's two years younger than I am, and certainly twenty years older and wiser*) had never flagged for a moment, even in the early growing-up years in Haylesburg when other brothers were busy beating each others' brains out. The friendship between them had been particularly unusual because, the neighbors had liked to say, no two brothers could have been more unlike. Jim was the shy one, often moody and lost in thought, not noticeably ambitious or overly eager to belong to a team. Tubby little Harry, on the other hand, was the amiable, outgoing one, with an instinctive talent for friendship, with an almost visible sandwich board around him that said he was going to go out and knock the world on its ear one day.

"Martha did phone you, as a matter of fact, at your office," Harry said accepting the drink and raising it in a toast, "and left a message. On Wednesday. But no answer."

"Damn it. There's RBS efficiency for you. I never got the message. Martha knows I would've called right back, doesn't she?"

"Sure," Harry chuckled, moving to the divan nearest the picture window. "Forget it. Nobody harbors any emotion around our menagerie for longer than a minute and a half. Not with five noses running at the same time. Say, I want to tell you about the show of yours last night. That Masscino fella came across so great I was tempted to call in and offer him a job at the shop. I guess he's got plenty of jobs lined up by now."

"So I hear," Jim nodded, joining him. "Tell me: what about the shop? Is there any business this time of year?"

"Could be better," Harry shrugged good-naturedly, "but then any business could be better. People don't look at their television sets much in the summertime—except for your program and The Late Show, so they don't bring their sets into my place for repairs. But the winter was very good, and I was able to send Martha and the Indians away for a couple of months, so who's going to believe a complaint if I wanted to make one?"

"I still think you're nuts," said Jim. "What do you pull in during a year in that two by four shop? Six? Seven?"

"Something like that."

"Which means you're nuts. Look, I've told you this a hundred times. This train I'm on is made of gravy, and with luck it'll stay the same way for a while. What're you struggling so damned much for when Fort Knox is right in your family?"

"Hey," Harry laughed, "I didn't take a death-defying cab ride all the way over here to sit for another lecture, Mr. Mellon. We've been all through this. I know that if I ever fall on my prat, I can call you. And don't think I won't."

"But in the meantime …"

"You just no spikka da English, do you?" Harry interrupted patiently, the grin becoming broader. "I'm above water, Jim. The family's getting good and fat, the Chevy still runs, and I don't owe anybody a nickel. Now let's cut out this poor-Harry crap and pick a fresher category."

The awesome thing, Jim observed, was that he meant it.

The visit promised, as always, to be far shorter than Jim wanted it to be. He kept trying to refill Harry's glass, repacking his plate with more of the elegant smoked turkey the Bonnerman sponsors had sent. But by two o'clock Harry maintained that he had nearly three hours of driving ahead of him, and Martha and the youngsters would raise hell if he showed up too late.

"Last night I went to bed with a girl from the office," Jim abruptly stated, amazed at the sharp, naked way it came out, amazed that he had planned to let it come out at all.

"So?" Harry remarked, blankly staring at him, obviously wondering what had prompted such an inappropriate, idiotic remark. "What're you looking for? A medal of honor?"

"It was more than a fast romp. I like the girl. It's probably going to develop into something."

He waited for a reply, a knowing or even unknowing blink of the eyes, something, anything. He had not meant to discuss it; he had never made a thorny point of burdening Harry with any of his personal problems. They had spent a quiet, happy hour together here in his new home and only three or four times had the image of Ginny Grant flashed before him. What the hell kind of nonsensical, grammar school blurting-out was this? To Harry, especially? Harry, who never preached sermons but who had made it clear more than once that he believed a married man had a strict, moral responsibility to keep away from other women?

"I'd better take that drink, after all," Harry directed, his usual smile gone. "But make it light on the whiskey."

"Nothing feels right. Nothing's building. I'm thirty-six years old and I have more than a man of thirty-six is supposed to have. And I can't see into next week."

Jim sat as far away from his brother as unnoticeably possible, placed his own second drink on the silver coaster beside him, and listened to the bottled-up words come out. He kept his eyes riveted in Harry's general direction, but suspected that he hadn't the guts to face him squarely.

"It was always this way with me," he went on, "going from one week to another without any deliberate plan for myself or anyone else. And yet there were the cross-purposes. Winning the day in debates and elocution contests, striving to get the lead in the senior play ... not the second lead but the lead, not because I actually wanted it but because for some insane reason I had to prove that I could start something and see it through, the way the old man never could. I had to keep proving it."

"Who to?" asked Harry.

"I don't know. Mom, I guess. God knows she never asked me to ... she was always too wrapped up in the old man, too absorbed in looking away from the fact that he was a failure by design and purpose to really care about either you or me."

Harry shook his head. "That isn't quite true. This is the age of blaming everything wrong with us, from losing our job to athlete's foot, on Lousy Old Mom. But you and I never had it quite that bad, Jim. Pa was selfish, sure, and—what do they call 'em in the textbooks—a compulsive dame chaser. But Mom loved us as much as she was able to. She never ran out on either of us. She was no Mother of the Year, but she gave us all she had in her to give."

"You felt that. I know. I never did."

"Than maybe you're partly to blame," Harry asserted gently, no anger in his voice. "There has to come a point in a man's life when he's got to chalk up what went before as the best that could've been under the circumstances, or experience, or some damn thing. What're you trying to get at—that you're taking up with a kid who has a cute rear and jollies you up because you figure your parents gave you a bum deal?"

"Because I feel empty."

"Hell. That was the old man's excuse, too, wasn't it, when he ran after every woman in Haylesburg and made Mom miserable? So what happened after all that chasing? Did it make him feel full?"

"What about you, Harry? Haven't you played around since you married Martha?"

Harry's jaw set and he regarded his light drink. "Yeah. Twice. Both times within the first year. We had $40 between us when we got married and we were both kids. I had that job with the furniture company in Newark and I didn't know from one day to the next whether I'd be in the Army or not. Six months after the wedding Martha got pregnant and the doctor said he heard two heartbeats. And I was lucky when I could afford an extra couple of cigars and the Sunday papers.

"That day the doctor said it might be twins I stopped off at a bar to get pie-eyed. This bimbo I wouldn't ordinarily look at twice sidles up to me and acts likes she's ready, willing and able, and I rented a hotel room for us. I remember the room cost me five dollars and I kept thinking all through it how many groceries I could've bought for five dollars." He finished his drink. "The second one was from a diner near Camp Blanding, right after basic training. She was a waitress named Isobel and she had this tattoo of a snake about an inch above her appendicitis scar. I took her out to a few cabarets and all she'd drink was Canadian whiskey, the expensive stuff. She took me to her place and I stayed there the weekend. And I kept wondering while I was making like some Don Juan, what the hell am I doing here with a stranger, kissing and undressing someone I don't know, and don't even much like …?"

"That was different," Jim said. "You were away from home. Most G.I.'s found someone like …"

"Yeah, yeah, I know the pitch. War, or business trip, or too much to drink at the country club justifies thumbing your nose at your marriage. And I was part of it. But that didn't make any of it right. And you're not playing it right, either, Jim. It's one thing when you're a kid and another thing when you're our age. Empty? What kind of hifalutin' alibi is that? Who doesn't feel empty sometimes?" He glanced at his watch. "I've got to beat it." He sat forward and asked, "How serious is this thing? You planning to divorce Fran?"

"That's been a possibility ever since we got married."

"Why just a possibility? If there was nothing between you two, why didn't you drop her early, when she would've had an easier time of landing a new husband? Why'd you make her hang on so?"

Jim studied his knuckles and felt restless again. "You don't think I'm very bright in the head, do you, Harry?"

"Well, I think you look for more trouble than you need to. But then, in one way or another, you've always done that, haven't you?" He got to his feet and set the glass on the coffee table. "If you feel *empty*," he said, bearing down harshly on the word, "maybe it's up to you to figure out why. I'm your friend as well as your brother, and I'm on hand whenever you need me, but I doubt if I can help you by banging you over the head. And I'm God-damned sure some little doxie who's just met you isn't going to help you either." Harry smiled again and extended his hand. "Now's the time for you to tell me to mind my own corny business."

"You know I listen to you, Harry," Jim said solemnly, sharing the handshake. "Maybe I did sound pretty corny myself."

"That's true. Maybe you did. By the way, the invite still holds. Any time you want to spend some time at the shore, we always have an extra cot."

"I know that. Thanks. One of these days the schedule will get a little less stiff."

"Okay. Now I have to drive out and settle a major crisis. Little Slugger's going to be five years old next week. Martha told me on the phone yesterday that he announced he hopes I get run over by a truck so he can marry her. That's what I call biting the hand that feeds you."

He waited until he heard the elevator open and close outside his door. He took the envelope with the number on it and walked anxiously to the kitchen phone. He finished dialing the seven digits and immediately hung up. Then he tapped the envelope over his knuckles, dialed again, and waited.

Standing erect, he counted eight long buzzes before he once more replaced the receiver.

The clock read twenty past two. Breathing heavily, he tore the envelope into shreds and dumped it all down the wall-incinerator.

While he was shaving, the penetrating ring from the bedroom made him nick his cheek. He dropped the razor and raced to his bed.

"Yes. Yes, hello."

"Jim, you fool. You sound out of breath," Monica Enders declared.

"Hello, Monica. How are you?"

"I swear I almost had to march on City Hall in order to get your private number; you were far harder to reach than my first husband, the Austrian Baron from Duluth, ever was; I'm not getting you out of bed or anything like that, am I?"

Ginny lost or mislaid my private phone number, he thought. *That's why she hasn't reached me. Who could she legitimately call to get my number?*

"No, wide awake. I want to thank you for that fine party."

"Actually, I should never talk to you again. You couldn't have been naughtier to me last night."

That kind of sticky talk had gone out with forehead tiaras and the perspiring duets from *The Student Prince*, he reflected. But he *had* been out of line. He hadn't really sought her out at the party.

"Naughty, Monica?"

"You did say good night to me before you left, but just at the moment that I was hip-deep in sales representatives from God-forsaken, Nebraska. That wasn't terribly kind of you and the least you can do is beg my pardon. I'd hoped to see a great deal more of you—afterwards."

Press down hard on the Creighton charm, he instructed himself. "Monica, I couldn't be more apologetic. Can I dry the dishes or take out the trash or something? It just didn't hit me that you really wanted to have a talk. Let me make it up to you somehow. Choose your weapons and I'm yours."

"My weapons are simple. Come see me tonight."

The sponsor's voice cooed and was right out of robin redbreast, with a scoop of tutti-frutti thrown in.

But it meant business.

"Let's say eleven o'clock," he suggested.

"Let's," she agreed, no longer Rebecca of Sunnybrook Farm. "The servant will be off to Tuscany to buy a bright new hat. I'll be wearing my own brand of cologne. Maybe something else, but I somehow doubt it."

CHAPTER NINE

A BUSINESS OFFICE on a Saturday afternoon in summer is the world's most depressing sight, but Jim entered his at a little past three with a forced upbeat of energy. For nearly two hours without help he made a dent in clearing part of his desk. He studied memos and backlog correspondence that had piled up, went over letters and phone messages with reference to past and future shows, sifted through the ideas for possible guests whom Evelyn and Bucky and Helene Masters had mentioned to him on paper. A lot of what had burgeoned into Stander-Creighton Enterprises had to be brought up to date personally, and he was happy that he could push aside all immediate pressures and face the large block of desk work on his own.

One wrinkled memo from Evelyn, dated four months ago, read *"What re show with Lee Gardiner? Grapevine says now a lush but did write Pelican St., pop novel, won last Samuel Boal Award. Ralph tells me Gardiner good bet, can talk, is personable, etc. Keep in mind."*

The number of personal letters was staggering. There were letters from all the boroughs, neatly typed and illegibly scrawled in pencil, crush letters and poisonous letters, letters telling him he was a menace to Christianity because he glorified gangsters and rapists, letters telling him he was an apostle of truth, the symbol of democracy in action, and the greatest guardian of the open forum in modern American history. Four letters were what the trade called the Honeybunch letters ("You're eyes and voice is the dreamiest on Tee-V. Who is you're favorite rock and Roll musical artist? Are you married & if so what does the 'lucky bride' call you in the privacy of your boudoir? Please send photo and autograp with you smiling").

A graduate honeybunch advised him she was 34, a divorcee, not hard on the peepers and, although she had never in her life ever done this before, he could come to visit her at her *own* (the word was underlined) apartment in the Bronx any night after his show but Saturdays. She enclosed her name and telephone number, with exhaustingly complete instructions on where to change subway trains, and which bus to take right to her corner after that.

There were the less extreme letters, too, the thoughtful, intelligent ones that commented on this interview or that one, and here and there offered effective pointers. They were the backbone letters, the ones that made him know his job was a useful one.

In the office background, the Big Brother of WRBS radio told him that Algeria was tottering, that Cabott Island had suffered a summer storm, and that a woman in the Red Hook section of Brooklyn had just murdered her taxi-driver husband because he hadn't liked the way she'd cooked his spaghetti ("Too much oregano!" he'd shouted just before she'd gone for the cleaver).

The scores upon scores of television interviews since January were all recorded here in the huge J.C. embossed album, the clinkers along with the great ones. And the great ones had made the bulk of the rat-race nearly worth while. Colter Small, the Haylesburg High English instructor, would have dropped his jaw in shock if he could have seen mopey Jim Creighton swap talk with an atomic scientist and a Shakespearian scholar, both in the same week.

When Herb Graham buzzed him that it was almost time to get down to The Tank for the six o'docker's rehearsal, Jim took care of the return calls. Bucky, as expected, bawled him out for taking so long to phone back and then leisurely drawled on about *Hot Spot* subjects which had either been discussed in detail between them many times, or could easily wait till Monday.

Evelyn Shoreham was vigorously, almost masculinely sorry about the atrocious behavior in Bucky's office yesterday; and would he forgive her? And, over this brutally long weekend would he feel free, if he felt lonesome, to visit her for a drink and a dinner, with absolutely no chiffon-strings attached?

"Thanks a lot, Evelyn," he replied, as courteously and unceremoniously as he could.

Between five and five-forty-five he made the segue between the wire service and the confab table with Herb and Clif Rawnsley, who had written up the skeleton for the newscast. He went on the air, loosening his necktie, holding the script in one hand and the necessary cigarette in the other, and knew within the first few minutes that he had more than a passable show. Occasionally he thought of Ginny Grant during the broadcast. She knew, of course, that he had this show on Saturday at six, and he hoped she would be listening.

At one point he came across the Victoria Falls dateline and called it Virginia Falls by mistake. Automatically he corrected himself. But during the break-in commercial from the tapes for the mint-flavored laxative, he wondered if she'd been listening, and if the slip meant anything to her.

By seven o'clock he was back at his stuffy apartment, lifting the receiver in anticipation, and asking the answering service if there had been any calls. There had been quite a few, yes, but none from her.

School-boy, he thought ruefully as he dropped his shirt and trousers over the nearest foyer chair and, deciding against food, built a liberal Vodka and ice.

Penrod 'n' Sam, he thought angrily as he carried the glass to the tufted chair closest to the largest window where he could prop his feet. *Huckleberry Finn. Huckleberry Lonchinvar. Huckleberry Dillinger. The next proper thing to do is to tug at the forelock and dig the toe into the sand.*

Harry, as always, had been right. You can scream for help, but you have to figure yourself out all by yourself. No one else can unscramble your eggs....

No whiskered farmer's shotgun had made him marry Frances Gerrick, the briefly-desirable brunette who had a lot more stickum to her, he'd suspected, than he'd had the time or willingness to give her credit for.

The Fifty-fourth Street doctor's findings (he advertised himself as a general practitioner on the men's room walls of side street cafeterias) had been conclusive. Jim Creighton, who had been told to have ambition but whose rubber arrows had been leading nowhere, had dug up a mild, far too urbane clergyman of no discernible denomination on First Avenue, and had married her.

"I now pronounce you man and wife," the clergyman had intoned, "and if you don't let me give the new missus the first kiss, then the whole proposition's null and void, like they say." The clergyman winked at his wife, who for some queer reason was loudly chewing gum.

They spent their wedding night in Fran's West Seventy-first Street walkup, looking at her snapshot album of faded photographs of her trip to the Grand Canyon and her kind Aunt Cora and her funny Nephew Michael. They drank Pepsi-Cola and ate bagsful of potato chips. He listened to her falteringly and formally explain that she wouldn't be sorry for anything because she would be the best wife he could dream of having.

It unsettled him to realize as he undressed in her cramped, shared bathroom, and skinned his knee as he struggled through the dark to join her in her trim single bed, that she was as attractive as she was, bumbling apologies and all. He felt inexorably Shanghaiied, but he found himself both touched and believing when, unasked, she went into a lengthy confession about never having been promiscuous; she had been alone and achingly lonely on that Christmas Eve, had needed attention, had been impressed with his nice manners and the fact that he hadn't said or done anything out of place even though he'd been a little high, and had invited him to take her home in a real taxicab because she'd sensed he wasn't one of those professional wolves. She had had one other love affair, she admitted, with a male stenographer named Harlan. It had gone strong for more than six months. But his mother had warned him that he should go to live back home with her in Great Neck because all unmarried girls were dirty and never went to church.

"I'll be a good wife, Jim, I promise," she muttered hoarsely in the blackness of night. "All my life I've been lonely, but now I've found you. I give you my word I'll be everything you want me to be."

They moved her pitifully few belongings down to his Bleecker Street one-and-a-half only because the Village apartment boasted its own bathroom and a little more closet space.

From time to time he would rouse himself from what he was sure had become a perpetual sleepwalking state to face the fact that he was going to be a father, and by a new wife who meant nothing to him. He didn't go out of his way to announce his marriage. His friends would drop in at the usual topsy-turvy Greenwich Village hours for a drink or an impromptu party, and he would introduce them—stiffly, humorlessly, he realized—to his wife. They were polite enough, but they made their exits without acceptance or understanding. Once, just after her belly had begun to swell, he met her in Radio City after work and they bumped into a tiresome girl who trilled that she was walking on air that day because she'd just received two tickets to the Perry Como television show.

"That was Jeannette," Fran informed. "She's about the best friend I have."

Fran lost the baby in the sixth month when she missed a step and fell down a flight of metal stairs leading to the Bleecker Street basement. Jim stayed home from work and as close to her as possible until the doctor assured him she'd be almost as good as new; she'd given her head a nasty bump and for a while there was a harrowing fear of a concussion, but the X-rays showed no such thing.

He could control neither the relief nor the guilt when it became clear that nothing was holding him, that he could get out. Fran was aware of the fresh possibility, of course, and could have opened it up for discussion, but she didn't. She had infuriated him from the start with an agonizing unwillingness to raise her voice to him, to fight with him, to openly question any of his motives or statements, or even to initiate any conversation more vital than whether or not they were running out of eggs or butter, unless he talked first.

The decision was sidestepped when Vic Perkey, the oldest member of the WRBS news desk, died, and the staff was reshuffled. Jim was advanced a notch, right into anchor man Gus Patterson's office. He was given a five dollar raise and what amounted to a nifty chance for advancement if Patterson—Rockland's equivalent of Ed Murrow—were to make him one of the personal office satellites. He worked harder than ever, not because he cared about becoming one of Gus Patterson's family of Brooks Brothers toadies, but because the others were giving him the You're-on-your-way-up wink and he imagined that it all was expected of him.

For long periods of time he could forget the sleepwalking marriage and the fact that sooner or later he would have to face up to it. He devised a kind of working shorthand with Fran, a way of living with her and sleeping in the same room with her and eating breakfast and dinner with her which would keep the marriage from either toppling or building. Through it, she seemed happy, content, foolishly grateful, as if no woman should expect any more than this. The thoughts of leaving her, of making a break from something stifling and boxed in, continued to grow in him. But he did nothing positive, took no decisive steps. In time, he told himself, it would work itself out....

The telephone's blatant jangle brought him sharply out of the past and to his feet. "Hello?" he cried to a silent line. The other person hadn't yet hung up. "Hello?" he repeated, narrowly restraining himself from calling her name.

Finally he set down the receiver. Once more the phone rang, imperiously now. Tensely he scooped it up. "Hello! Who is that?" he commanded but this time, without hearing a click, there was the steady low hum of the free line. He dialed for the operator and told her what had happened, although he could have recited verbatim her report that no records were ever kept of incoming calls.

It was getting late—Monica Enders never liked to be kept waiting by anyone—but he took his time at pouring another Vodka; if it *had* been Ginny, she probably would call back. He downed the drink and kept the bathroom door wide open while he took his second shave and shower for the day, and he polished off the drink as he dressed. The apartment was still mute.

The fact was repulsive to him as he finished dressing that he spent so much of his life doing things he wasn't equipped or eager to do. The Enders visit, for instance. What would have happened if he'd told her this afternoon that he'd be busy? Or that his wife was expected back in town? Or, by God, that business was one thing and his time after working hours was another? Sure, why not the truth? What would she do—or anyone else, for that matter—if he made a simple public announcement that he wanted to slow down on everything before he blew his top? Enders and the other sponsors were selling their products. The press agents and the lobbyists for the knotheaded tap dancers were being treated right. Fat Red was getting revenue. Bucky Stander wasn't about to go on relief.

He was the hottest thing of the year. Why did everyone know it except Jim Creighton?

Before he left, he dialed his answering service and decided against leaving word that he could be reached at Monica Enders'. Instead, he said he would phone back from time to time.

The July late evening was placid and pleasurable. On Sutton Place, dowagers and hookers, one camp indistinguishable from the other except for age, were out with their men or their families of chihuahuas. Although the starched doormen were on duty, most of the lights in the swanky apartment buildings were out, which meant that business would be good for the second-story boys on this holiday-weekend night.

At Forty-fourth he stopped off at Costello's for a lubrication that might make the opening hellos at Enders' a trace more bearable. Halfway through his drink at the bar, Steve Lobeck, the *New York Dispatch* television columnist who had been after Jim's neck from the beginning of *Hot Spot*, strolled in with a spectacularly gaudy blonde and nodded chummily as they sat in a booth. Jim nodded soberly back and turned his head. *The semi-literate bastard*, he thought.

"Mr. Creighton, Mr. Lobeck would like you to join him at the table," a waiter advised him at the bar. "For a drink."

"Tell him no."

"Right. Can I kick the son of a bitch's head off while I'm at it?"

"Sure," Jim grinned. "But only if he talks back." That helps a little, he thought. A mean bastard is judged by the calibre of people who hate him. And the waiters at Costello's are the salt of the earth.

Maybe he should have gone after a summit meeting with Lobeck shortly after the start, when the former third-string movie reviewer had become a full-fledged TV critic, and had seldom let a column pass without writing that *Jim Creighton's Hot Spot* was a witless, irresponsible show which served as the perfect soapbox for degenerates, subversives and, worst of all, thinkers. No other reviewer had pummeled at him so thoroughly, so naggingly, so like the school bully who's just taken over the classroom stiletto concession. More than once, after reading an especially nasty few paragraphs which had had little if anything to do with the preceding night's show, Jim had bridled and wanted to find out what gave. Bucky had calmed him down each time, with the assertion that Lobeck was itching for a fight that would get his circulation going, and that the smartest thing to do was to pretend not to notice.

The almost aimless knifings, as regular as nervous tics, hadn't hurt the show or him of course; certainly Fat Red, who was known to read every television reviewer as religiously as he read the Scriptures, had never said a word about Lobeck's apparent thirst for blood. But, Jim recalled uneasily, there was something else. Lobeck was never wholly satisfied to jump on a show alone; he also felt himself called upon to be the guardian of television's morals.

Jim paid his tab and started down the aisle toward the door. "Hey there, stuck-up!" Lobeck called cheerfully as he approached the table. "Hold your horses a while and say hello!" He was nearly as tall as Jim. But there was a waxen, emaciated look about him that summoned up images of an unventilated crematorium.

"Sorry. I'm in a hurry."

"Aw, relax, soldier," Lobeck enthused, chuckling, and reached out for him. The play was big. There wasn't a doubt in the world that he was intent on putting on an impressive show for the blank-eyed, voluptuous young tart across from him. "We've been in the same game for quite a spell now and I haven't even had the chance to shake hands yet. I want you to meet Miss Mindy Spears. Maybe you'd be interested in getting her on your show some night. You know, a plug never hurts. Miss Spears is a terrific vocalist, gonna be a lot bigger than those neat little nigger singers you've been selling for so long."

"Very please'a meet'cha, Mr. Cramer," Miss Spears percolated, sitting back and taking a deep, skillfully rehearsed breath to show that she was not a boy.

"Uh—my hand's getting tired, Jimmy," Lobeck volunteered, still cheery, but somehow not getting the point that his offer of friendship wasn't being picked up. Then a suave frost covered his voice. "You're going to shake it, aren't you?"

Jim frowned, not sure he understood. "Let me try to figure out something," he said. "What's all this about? You've done everything you could to low-rate my work, but now you want me to shake your hand. Why?"

Lobeck blinked, and then laughed derisively. "Now there's a sensitive soul for you! You think that in my position as a television critic I ever had anything personal against you, Jimmy?

Heck, I'm a working stiff like you. Why would you want to talk like that? I'm a television critic on one of the top notch papers in ..."

"Save the nice, crunchy self-applause for your *chanteuse* here, Lobeck ..."

"Lis-sun," Miss Spears objected, breathing again. "I don't approve of bad words in mixed company!"

"... and get off my backside with this phony pal talk. I have about as much interest in shaking your hand as I do in laying a wreath over Hitler's grave. Write all the sour-grape garbage you like about my program, but don't try to buddy me. Now please excuse me."

Swiftly Lobeck was leaning toward the edge of the booth seat, unready to let him go just yet. Flustered because he obviously had planned to give himself the big man treatment in front of the girl, he half rose now and grabbed at Jim's coattail.

"You're yammering for a handout, Creighton, that's all, just like all the ninety-day wonders in this business. I'll give you one more chance. You apologize to Miss Spears here for talking out of turn or I swear to God I'm going to really go after you in my paper. I know, for instance, why you had to get married ..."

The feel of the hand on his jacket blinded Jim with a fury he had not imagined possible. He swatted the hand away, making the action as unobserved as he could by Costello patrons, and stepped back to quietly shove Lobeck against the wall and sit beside him.

"Listen good, you vicious son of a bitch," he warned softly, his eyes blazing into Lobeck's. "I'm not beating the crap out of you here and now only because Tim is a great gentleman and a friend of mine and I stay clean in a friend's place. If you want to tangle, then let me know right now. I can wait for you outside. Let me know now."

"I'm not interested in …"

"Then that's your answer. You're a coward. Now hear me out," Jim said, his words racing like the wind, "and your tramp vocalist here is invited to listen, and you can pass the word on to all the other sucker fish. I don't know what goes on in your pointed head when you set yourself up as a critic of your peers. But I'll lay this on you: don't you ever try to pull rank on me again, for as long as you write that half-ass column. A TV show comes across or it doesn't. That's your job to say. Whether a performer has the wrong color or wrong spouse or wrong mistress isn't."

"Oh, I get it," Lobeck said, stuttering slightly, his face ashen. "It's the old story. When a performer flubs, it's the critic who's wrong."

"Listen better, punk. If you ever say or write or infer one word about my wife, than you'd better start running back into the woodwork. Because I'll find you, you sick bastard. I'll find you and with these hands I'll kill you." He could feel his own breathing come more heavily, and he was astonished that he'd managed to give the impression that no threat of violence was in operation in this booth.

Gradually, as Miss Spears' button eyes tore about the room and as Lobeck sent up every flag to show he was frightened, Jim sat away and unclenched his grip from the columnist's arm.

"Do we understand each other now?" Jim demanded.

Steve Lobeck shook his shoulders to unruffle his pretty suit and forced a weak new chuckle at the girl. "I thought that Humphrey Bogart was dead. I guess I was wrong." He glared at Jim. "You've spoken your cute little piece, Grand Inquisitor. I tried to be a friend but you put up the 'don't disturb' sign. The biggest-rated people in TV take off their hat when they see Lobeck coming, but you're bigger than they are. Okay with me. Copasetic. You're excused from the class room."

A fresh urge to crush his right fist into Lobeck's jaw flooded through Jim, but he contained it. He returned the glare and strode out, fervently wishing that the writer would decide to follow, and he even waited outside for a few minutes before he headed for Monica Enders' penthouse. He felt dazed and unfulfilled, and knew one thing for sure: if Bucky ever found out he had talked back to a newspaper writer, there would be everlasting hell to pay.

It was considerably past ten when he arrived at Monica's corner, and he knew what was to come. The light blue (or was it light red in these, the modem times?) diaphanous dressing gown. The peremptory chastisement for his being late and keeping her waiting, with a liberal usage of words such as *naughty* and *gwathous thakes* and *oojums boojums* to make him feel doubly guilty. The drink all prepared, a jigger of Scotch and a ton of ice. An ostentatiously atonal clatter of Bartok or Schoenberg from the phonograph, with the guarantee of wall-kicking cymbals and kettle-drums at just a little before midnight. The husbands who hadn't understood her. The gown parting at just the right angle, at just the right time, as shrewdly as if it had been trained to roll over and play live by Pavlov.

I don't want it, he thought.

I'm here, he thought.

He entered a nearly dosing drug store for a pack of cigarettes and padded to the rear telephone booths. He dialed the answering service.

"Jim Creighton," he said. "Anything?" An obese woman sat in a wicker chair outside his booth, her lips going in noiseless talk. She wore a green eyeshade over her forehead and her fingers tickled an obese cat's throat.

"One call," the girl from the service disclosed. "She said her name was Ginny."

"Yes," he said, sitting up.

The girl repeated her phone number. "She called in at nine-forty-two. Says it's important. Wants you to call her as soon as possible."

He called and she picked up her receiver on the first ring.

"Ginny …"

"Oh, Jim. Is it Jim?" Her voice was hoarse, strained, and he knew she was crying.

"Yes," he replied. At first it seemed important, somehow, to intimate indifference, to punish her for taking so long. But then there was the weeping, the hysterical, uncontrollable weeping, and he was convinced that her reason for silence had been legitimate.

"Darling, I—"

"What is it, Ginny?" he demanded imperatively, getting as dose as he could to the telephone's mouthpiece.

"Are you terribly busy? Can you come here right away?"

"Yes. Yes, of course. What is it?"

"After you left," she said, "afterwards … he came up. He followed us. He was outside all the time you were here. He—he came up. With a knife."

"Who? Who was it, Ginny?"

"Lee …"

"What happened?"

"Darling. Please hurry."

"Yes, darling. Right away. I'll be there in fifteen minutes. Try to …"

"It was dreadful. He was going to—I thought he was going to kill me …"

"Hang up. I'll be there as soon as I can find a taxi."

He rushed out to the sidewalk and hailed a free cab going in the opposite direction. Rushing for it, he jumped in the back seat and snapped, "Cornelia Street. And here's an extra twenty if you can get through the lights in a hurry."

Ginny's door was bolted as he raced up the stairs. She was reluctant for a moment to believe it was he in the hall, but finally she admitted him.

She wore the same things she had worn when he'd left her. Her hair was straggly and what was left of her lipstick was dully streaked. She rushed to him, clutched at his body as she shivered, and breathed, "It's—so dangerous for you to be here. He says he's going to kill you, too."

CHAPTER TEN

"ARE YOU ALL RIGHT?" Jim insisted, carrying her to the couch. "Did he hurt you?"

"I didn't mean to get you involved in it ..."

"Stop it. Tell me what happened."

The tears welled up again and she was unable to speak for several minutes. Shuddering with what had to be a fresh recollection of fright, she refused to free herself from him. Jim sat on the edge of the couch, squeezing her arm protectively, assuring her she was safe, that he would stay, that he would be here for as long as she wanted.

The front room lent the hideous impression of violence. Papers were strewn about the floor and one of the small bookcases had been turned over. The Venitian blind was drawn as before, but now two of the slats were broken in half; Jim peered through and noticed that a tiny part of the window pane had been broken. The shade was missing from the floor lamp, giving the room a smeared, underwater glow.

Presently Ginny seemed to get hold of herself, although her right hand continued to press into his wrist. Only when she took the white handkerchief from his breast pocket and blew her nose did he notice the ugly bruise under her chin. He touched it and Ginny drew back, wincing slightly. "He beat you," Jim said.

"I've known him for so long," she confided slowly, quietly, forcing containment. For some odd reason she appeared to find it difficult to meet his searching eyes. "I told you about him. You met him. Yes, that's right, you met him. You called him the onion peeler. And that's what he was. The sweetest, most harmless boy in the world. How could he have had such—anger in him?"

"Let me get some warm water and swab that bruise," Jim urged, gently releasing himself and starting to get off the couch. "It'll make you feel better—"

"No," she stressed quickly, sitting up. "No, please."

"All right, Ginny. I'm here. I won't go away." He lighted a cigarette and placed it between her lips. "You said on the phone that he was outside all the time I was here."

"He knocked at the door about ten minutes or so after you left. I wasn't expecting anyone else. I thought it was you coming back. I ... I was hoping it was you coming back, I discovered the minute you went out. He forced his way in. At first he was the same mild, harmless Lee, and I tried to humor him because he seemed to be only a little drunk. Then he began making these horrid, obscene accusations about you and me. It was—it was so awful, so pitiful to hear—those terrible words, like a small boy being bad because he wants to be noticed."

She took a deep drag at the cigarette. "I couldn't have imagined what was going to happen next. He hit me. He doubled his fist and punched me. I fell back ... I must have screamed ... and he took out this knife. I remember that I was more fascinated than scared for a moment, as though it all belonged in some old Boris Karloff movie. Or in one of those tracts about juvenile delinquents. It was a silly, typically Hollywood kind of knife with an immense blade and somehow, for a minute or so even after he hit me, the whole thing seemed too ludicrous, too fourth-reelish, to really frighten me. Then he hit me again and threatened to kill me because I'd been unfaithful to him. It was so ... remarkable, those words coming from Lee. In his book he went so out of his way to spurn all the obvious cliches, and there he was, telling me that if he couldn't have me, no one else ever would. That first he'd disfigure me and then murder me."

"He was here through the night?"

"All night and all through today. Till—six o'clock or so, I guess. I can remember his storming out of here—which was absolutely crazy in itself, because he must have drunk up most of the liquor there in the kitchenette—and I can remember running to the telephone to call you, and then stopping because it seemed so ridiculous to try to involve you in my troubles. Anyway, I didn't make it. I fainted. I came to at about half-past nine. I went to lock the door, and that's when I became really scared. I thought about calling the police, but I couldn't bring myself to do it. I phoned you."

"You poor baby."

"Darling, I've done wrong, haven't I?" she implored, bringing her palms to his cheeks. "I swear I didn't mean to make you a part of my life to this sordid extent. I had no designs on you, no serious designs at the start. When you went away from me this morning I knew I was in love with you, but I still had no intention of setting my cap for you, or expecting you to seriously care. But I kept thinking of you while he was here—once, this afternoon, when I thought he'd passed out, I dialed your number and he made me hang up—I wanted only you. Oh, I'm sounding like such a tiresome character out of *East Lynne*."

"It was right for you to call me, Ginny. I haven't thought of a thing but you since I left here. I went through seventeen kinds of hell when you didn't phone at noon. If it's possible to use such a creaky, shaky word as 'love' after only a day, I love you."

When she responded, as a little girl who's been in the cookie jar responds when she's told there will be no spanking, Jim Creighton brought her into his arms and kissed her. He kissed her newly, sweetly, in a cleansed way he could not have thought last night he was capable of giving to her.

Gradually he rose, moved dizzily to a washcloth in the bathroom, soaked it in warm water, and returned to her with it. Tenderly he freshened the tautness from her face and kissed her again. He lifted her from the couch and carried her to her bedroom. He disrobed her, found a virginal nightgown in her bureau and dressed her in it, as carefully and gently as he would attend to a needy child. He went back to the kitchenette, warmed some milk for her, and sat with her while she sipped it. He stayed until she fell asleep, her wonderful body curling up, her thumb going automatically over her lips.

Returning to the kitchenette, he found an unopened bottle of Scotch which Gardiner had evidently overlooked, and poured himself a long drink. Downing the first half of it, he was conscious of the bitter tension in his tired body, of the crippled muscles that pleaded exhaustion. Suddenly he remembered Monica Enders, and instinctively he looked toward the telephone next to Ginny's bed. Perhaps she would still be waiting. Certainly she would be cursing him. He weighed the rightness of calling her, of making up some elastic excuse that would get him out from under. But there was no way of going to the telephone without wakening Ginny.

Somberly he finished the stiff drink and watched his still-nervous hands pouring another.

Gardiner, the sweet smiling son of a bitch, had used her sexually. Ginny hadn't said so, but it was clear. He had abused her with threats and a knife and he belonged at the bottom of the Hudson River. *Then why weren't the cops called in?* he asked himself. *Their business is to go after the Gardiners, isn't it?*

I should call them now, he thought. *But I'm standing here as usual, trusting as usual that the important ships will keep passing in the night and will never stop to destroy me or anyone close to me.*

The police come in and ask questions. They ask questions of a television interviewer named Jim Creighton, who is the biggest thing in New York City since Rapid Transit, and who soon will become the most glamorous male name around the country's twenty-one inch screens. The newspapers pick up the story. And the Lobecks reach into the desk's bottom drawer and pull out the old time headlines that include scorchers like Love Nest and Adulterer.

And that is the soggy end of Jim Creighton.

Bringing the bottle and the double old-fashioned glass to the front room, Jim glanced into the semi-darkened bedroom. She was sleeping peacefully, her bosom rising and falling evenly under the single light bedsheet. Her little fingers had crowded into a fist and their knuckles rested against her mouth. One lovely bare leg had escaped from the imprisonment of the sheet, and rested nakedly above it.

It made sense to go to her again, but instead he padded back to the couch, aware that he would get drunk tonight. That was the way his father would have handled the situation, wasn't it? He shrugged out of his jacket, dropped his necktie to the rug, and collapsed to the couch cushions.

You have to figure yourself out all by yourself, Harry had told him today ...

The Creighton boys were born, two years apart, in a prosperous factory town twenty-four miles east of Pittsburgh. Haylesburg, Pennsylvania, rarely housed more than 17,000 people, even in its boom years, but the town fathers proclaimed, and perhaps rightly, that it was a wealthier junior city than any other of its junior city competitors in that part of the state. If you were ambitious and wore a white shirt and could work yourself up to getting the Chamber of Commerce to call you by your fist name, there was no reason why you couldn't find a way to open your own shop and watch it thrive. If you were a working man and weren't afraid to get your hands dirty, as The Rotary delighted in repeating, Haylesburg was overflowing with job offers.

Andrew Creighton, whose family was one of the two oldest in town, was an Elk, Shriner, Moose, and was in the front row at every Fourth of July oration at Mt. Kirby Park. He never entirely understood which camp would best make use of his talents—the ambitious white shirt camp or the working man camp. Twice he opened his own haberdashery and twice he failed. Eventually he became a clerk at the better of the two local department stores, The Vanity ("We Beat Pittsburgh Stores in Both Style & Price!"), and, by the time the boys were in grammar school, had become section manager of the men's shoe department. The advancement involved a $15 weekly raise, a blood-red rose in his lapel, and the right to bully hell out of his two assistants. He was tall, flat bellied, handsome, with a round and florid face that made his wife think of Warren Harding, and he had a fierce though discreet urge to make a sexual play for every woman he met.

When they were still very young, both Jim and Harry were conscious, sometimes embarrassingly so, of their father's drive to be The Haylesburg Don Juan, as he sniggeringly grew to be called in the town's pool rooms and diners. Harry was the kid who early had busied himself in The Scouts and The Y and basketball at school, and who came home only to eat and sleep; he was friendly with both his parents, but all his interests lay outside the home. Jim, on the other hand, a swiftly growing, too moody kid for Haylesburg, made himself more and more available to his mother's needs for company and understanding, and stayed close to her during those fearful interludes when Dad went out on a toot and showed up drunk and with lipstick dramatically smeared over his collar.

While Harry seemed oblivious to everything tortuous that was going on at home, Jim realized that he hated his father, the same man who had so patiently taught him to stand on roller skates and how to protect himself against a fast left. "You're all I have, Jimmy." His mother wailed again and again when Dad abruptly decided to stay away from home. "You're my life, my hope, my protection. I'd never tell this to Harry in a billion years, but you're my favorite. Yes, you are. You're my real flesh and blood and you understand me. Don't ever leave me."

Then there would be signs of the old man's coming out of what Mother had come to call "That old craziness," and he would deliver a bunch of roses and automatically re-establish himself as the head of the household. Mother would adore him once more and neglect her sons. Jim found himself blinking at the sudden switch of affections, and hated the fact that night after night, while Harry snored happily away, he suffered a continual insomnia, the kind that sent him kicking at covers, wrestling with pillows, and sullenly rising from bed after nine hours with only two or three solid hours of sleep. That old craziness was over, his parents were billing and cooing; and why wasn't he getting better grades at school?

"What're you messing with that Milton and Keats junk for, Jim?" Harry asked him once. "We need a guy who can make a basket without getting on an elevator, and you're twice the size of any guy on the team. What do you say?"

"What're you, bats in the belfry or something?" Jim scorned. "With all that's going on at home? Do you really expect me to go out with Mom sitting home like that all by herself? Somebody has to take care of her. You and the old man sure don't care too much."

Harry graduated from high school and left Haylesburg, not asking his father for a cent or a blessing. He went to New York, where all the rebels went after high school, got a job as a salesman in Newark, New Jersey, and fell in love with and married a Jewish girl named Martha Plotkin. The old man, who loved to get loaded and tell The Elks that his family had been in America long before Benjamin Franklin, regularly suggested that the Negroes be sent back to Africa, that all Catholics were foreign agents, and that International-Capitalist-Communist Jews should also be deported to Africa, venomously carried on for a week. The pure strain would be broken, he cried, and it had been his wife's fault for encouraging this Jew kind of stuff from her boy, when her rightful attention belonged to her husband, whose family had been here longer than Benjamin Franklin's.

Unlike Harry, Jim felt himself constrained to stay in Haylesburg, although Grover Weaver, who had given him a part time job on the local radio station, had advised him that he should try his wings in *New York* radio. His mother's game of now-hate now-love for Andrew Creighton continued, unchangingly, as the old man occasionally made a strike with a new Haylesburg girl and stayed away for nights at a time.

It continued even when the old man, at 55, was found in the bed of what was called a daisy at three in the morning by her common-law husband who worked nights. The man rustled through his bureau, picked up a shotgun, and shot the old man in the shoulder.

The juice of it got in The Haylesburg Daily News, and Andrew Creighton was fired from his job. He wept in jail for his wife and she came running. Jim knew it was time to go. He had fought to overcome his shyness and his lack of desire to forge ahead by plunging into one project after an other because his mother had wanted him to, between bouts with her own interests. He finally saw and heard the meat of the meaning of his years in this town, and accepted Grover Weaver's letters of recommendation to the New York station. As his father wailed for help, and his mother rushed to give him help, Jim Creighton boarded a bus for New York.

"I'm going, Mom," he had said.

"Oh, please don't, Jimmy," she had pleaded. "I don't want you to."

"What can I do here?" he'd asked hopefully.

"You can do everything," she'd answered. "Daddy's fine now and he needs me. But you can never tell when he'll get That Old Craziness again. And I'll need you more than ever then."

The bus delivered him to Manhattan the very next day.

Jim finished the bottle of Scotch in Ginny Grant's living room and staggered to her bed after he switched off all the lights. She revived slightly and reached out for him as he slid in beside her. He kissed her again and her bare arms possessively encircled him.

I never meant to get involved past a night, he thought. *The professional leeches had a hundred girls available to help get me over the lonely, rocky weekends. But I wasn't interested.*

And now, whether I like it or not, I have a woman. And she will never make demands or work to cause me trouble. But there will be trouble.

And over the period of a night, I am up to my neck.

CHAPTER ELEVEN

GINNY WAKENED HIM on Sunday morning with a steaming glass on a saucer. The radio next to the bed was playing a cozy nighttime instrumental. The holiday-weekend rain had come back, but it was gentler now, not nearly so driving as it had been on Friday. The scent of her tangy perfume was pleasurably heavy in the room.

"Me loyal Jap gull," she declared as he grinned and sat up. "Me bling master his bleakfast, tly to make him ploud of me."

"Master velly ploud," Jim nodded. There was not the vaguest hint that anything unhappy had ever happened to her. Exuberance seemed to be radiating from every pore. She wore a candy stripe blouse, the top three buttons undone, and a skin tight, vigorously red pair of leotards that accented the flawless curves of her legs and thighs. A wide ribbon, also candy-striped, pony-tailed her soft yellow hair. Her eyes were clear, her face was young and flushed and alive, her makeup was perfect, and the chin bruise was, queerly, now hardly noticeable.

"Drink this before it goes all lukewarm and mooshy," she instructed, sitting beside him. "If you needed hair on your chest, this would do it."

"It's a deadly potion, isn't it?" Jim inquired, amiably feeling more refreshed than he had ever felt before. "It'll turn me into a toad, won't it?"

"Not till the stroke of midnight. It's a bullshot."

"My Lord," he said, taking it. "What's that?"

"Sort of my own recipe. I'm known as Betty Crocker Grant around the *Good Housekeeping* crowd. It's a bouillon cube, Worchestershire sauce, salt, pepper, and a shot of the dog's hair. It's guaranteed to knock your hat off and then clear the sinuses. But you have to drink it fast."

"Yes ma'am," he nodded obediently and drank it down. Bullshot is right! he thought; *this is potent medicine.* But it went down beautifully. "I feel like that guy from *White Cargo*, the one with the pith helmet. And you make a mighty tempting Tondelayo." He touched her arm. "Let's have a kiss on it."

"Uh uh," Ginny laughed, backing away. "Your eggs and bacon are on the stove. We ploud native gulls never allow pleasure to mix with business. Now finish that and change the station if you like. There are cigarettes in the box right next to the radio."

It was all goofy, he thought as he watched her stride out of the room, humming a snatch from the *Boat Dat's Leavin' For New York* piano solo on the radio. She'd gone through at least half a day of the worst indignity that can happen to a woman, and now she was—well, glowing.

In the bathroom, as he waited for the breakfast, he took a critical look at himself in the wall mirror and was glumly satisfied that his face resembled a game of jacks. Why had he needed to knock off an entire bottle last night all by himself, and what time had he finally stumbled to bed? Still, he didn't feel too overly racked with pain, and obviously she didn't care how he looked. He found some Lavoris, squished it around in his mouth, and limped back to bed, again overwhelmed by his happiness and the fact that for spaces of time he could blot out most of yesterday's nightmare.

The breakfast was crisp, hot, and delicious. Ginny shared his tray with her own plate and ate with him. The marvelously mellow coffee immediately reminded him of Mrs. Wentsmann, who had defended the warmed-over varnish she called coffee as the delight of Herr Groeter's mornings.

"There's plenty more of everything, if you're still hungry," Ginny advised.

"Not another drop," he said. "That bullshot of yours has me purring like a Tiger cub."

The apartment had been cleaned to spotlessness. The book case had been put back in place, the blind had been raised, the lampshades had been righted, and the whole atmosphere was one of fresh breath. They made love after breakfast, earnestly and innocently, meeting one another as though for the first time and the thousandth time, warmly, breathlessly, patiently, greedily. He dimly recalled that he had made odd statements last night about love and of never leaving her, and it occurred to him now that he meant them, that he had never meant anything so much in his life. The hell with Wally Brunow's back fence gossip, he thought. *For the very first time I feel the wholeness of myself. I do love her. She is right and real and there is no reason on earth why this must end when the weird summer ends.*

"Ginny," he said aloud.

"What?" she asked, surprised.

"Ginny. I just felt like saying your name. I love to say your name."

"Do you know I love you very much? Do you know I can say that now without thinking that something up in the skies will send a thunderbolt down here and strike me dead? Do you know how comfortable it is for me to tell you I love you?"

"It's strange, isn't it, everything about us? Suddenly we're very comfortable with each other. We can show our vaccinations without blushing."

Her eyes bore into his as she nodded in agreement. "It *is* a little eery, isn't it? I come from a background that dictates that a girl mustn't be forward enough to ever shake hands with a suitor until they've gone on dates—well chaperoned—for at least a year. A well brought up girl was expected to make noises like early Scarlett O'Hara and to regard lust as some kind of Yankee emotion that was to suddenly switch on after the wedding, if ever. I had this banged into my head from the moment I discovered the difference between girls and boys. It's awfully hard to divorce yourself from your upbringing, even if the upbringing, was flukey."

"Yes, I know."

"All this came from my mother, really. Not my father. Never my father. He was the kindest, most perfect and understanding man in the world. Do you mind terribly if I talk about him? I sort of got sidetracked, but it all fits in."

"I want to hear everything about you, Ginny."

"Daddy would have been president of the United States if he'd lived long enough. I'm sure of it. He was the mayor of our town for three consecutive terms and he made his living as an undertaker. He cried a lot. He was the most manly man that ever lived, but when a friend of his in town died and the corpse was brought to him, he cried, sometimes for hours on end. My mother never understood him at all, that he had a right to be as freely emotional as he was. She came from the fancy Cartwrights, and they believed that anyone who showed any feelings at all, woman or man, was a social disgrace. She was the one who tried to put all that butterfly netting in my brain about how men were such base, lustful, weak creatures, and the only chance a woman had to survive was to keep proving that she was better than both the man and the ape. That you were supposed to hold your true colors in, that men went all to seed if they even thought you had feelings on a par with theirs.

"You don't know my mother," Ginny went on. "She's very charming and very persuasive and the wickedest woman that ever lived. She killed Daddy. He was thirty-six years old and in the prime of life, but he had one weakness. She threw these phony migraine headaches and stomach pains and faints every time he made a move to make a teeny forward step in politics, and she demanded that he spend all his time pampering her. He committed suicide. He couldn't take the gaff any longer. He took a pistol out of his desk drawer one night and put the butt of it in his mouth and killed himself. I don't blame him for a minute. I would have done the same thing, if I'd been as saintly as he was. I wouldn't have slogged through this miserable world if I'd had someone like her to contend with every time I turned around. Would you? Wouldn't you prefer his way out? Speaking realistically?"

The anxiousness of the plea made Jim uneasy. "I doubt it, Ginny. Every man considers suicide from time to time, I guess, but he never takes his own life simply because a woman doesn't love him. I'm sure it's a great deal more complicated than that."

"Then you don't understand. Daddy wouldn't have done it otherwise. He was too fine, too dear, too sensitive to be treated the way she treated him, with all her Cartwright strict rules and bylaws. If he'd had a woman who recognized him, who honestly knew every fibre of his body, every cell of his brain, do you think he'd be dead now? My wonderful, wonderful father?"

"Ginny," Jim said, wishing she were as simple and sprightly as she had been when she'd brought that hodge-podge of a soup to him in bed. "You're a girl of great intelligence. Do you truly believe a man is ever destroyed by a woman if he doesn't want to be? Do you?"

A frown wrinkled her forehead. Her face showed a fleeting anger as she regarded him, as if she'd never regarded him before.

"Certainly I do believe it," she snapped emphatically. "No man can cross the street by himself or even blow his own nose without the help of a woman. I believe it as surely as I believe that women have the right to vote."

There were no more pressures left hanging in the air, after a while. The day whipped by relaxedly, bathed in love and good humor. After Jim showered, Ginny had a man-sized drink waiting for him and managed in some unseen way to keep refilling his glass without making him aware that she had left him for a second. She talked about herself because he asked her to and because he was interested in listening to her talk. He prodded her about Lee Gardiner, and she detailed it again, this time as though he had been here a year ago, not last night.

They had never been intimate with one another in all the time they'd been together, Ginny confessed, simply because she'd never seen him as anything more than a good friend who could be counted on to be a friend when she wanted one. Lee had frozen with fear after the unexpected success of his novel, and began to drink with dedicated desperation; she had struggled to help him find himself again, because she knew how very much talent he had, but he stubbornly refused to be found. Obviously he had come to misunderstand her interest for love, and had gone berserk last night when she'd shown attention to Jim. Through the long day he had brandished that knife, drunk more and more, talked like a madman about how no one could stop him from capturing the castle, and had repeatedly made stumbling advances at her.

No, he had not succeeded. He had not been able to, she said.

"Will he be back, do you think?" asked Jim.

"No, somehow I don't think so," Ginny replied. "And isn't it funny, I wouldn't be frightened any more if he did come back.

I guess I never really thought he would use that knife. Not Lee. If he's sobered up by now, I'm positive he's the most mortified little boy on the face of the earth."

Jim learned a great deal about Ginny Grant during the too-fast-moving afternoon, paradoxical and self-contradicting things now and then, to be sure, but only because she seemed to be as conscious as he of the heartless way that time rushed by, and she wanted to say as much as possible before he would have to leave her.

His watch read two o'clock. Then, only minutes later, he read it again and it was a quarter past five. He blinked, unbelievingly. He checked with her and she confirmed that, indeed, it was a quarter past five.

"Damn it," he complained. "I have to be out of here forty-five minutes ago. I'm supposed to be at the studio at five-thirty."

"Oh, no!" Ginny groaned. "You didn't say anything!"

"That *Butcher, Baker* panel show at seven. I thought of it hours and hours ago and then promptly put it out of my mind." Jim rose from the couch and realized with sharp dread that he was far more wobbly than he felt. Her constant servings of Scotch certainly hadn't helped. His brain felt cobwebby when he thought of himself being called upon to ad-lib and be chipper in precisely an hour and three-quarters from now. "Oh, man," he moaned, "but I'm sure not ready to take on the network."

"Maybe you can get out of it," she suggested.

He began to search for his tie and shoes. "You make ze beeg joke. Do me a favor, will you? Heat up some strong black coffee for me in a hurry while I try to patch myself together."

"Yes, of course," Ginny said and hurried to the stove.

What got into me? he thought derisively. *I've never allowed myself to have more than one belt, before a show. Why did I let it slip my mind?* He was fleetingly alarmed to find that he couldn't walk with an easy, straight gait to the bathroom. He regarded her shower for a moment and suspected that a few minutes under the cold, pricking needles would revive him. But there wasn't time. He washed his face and the nape of his neck with cold water and tried to remember if he had a change of clothing at his office; he could get by on camera with what he was wearing now, but the slacks were baggy and his white shirt looked as though it had been stepped on.

The coffee was ready when he reappeared and he gulped it down as he noted the time again. "Any idea where the best place is to find a taxi?" he inquired.

"Try the corner of West 4th. Probably the subway would be a lot faster than a cab, but this is Sunday, and if you miss one you'll have to wait forever for another one. Oh, darling, I'm so sorry you have to rush out this way. Can I see you later? Can you come back? Can I meet you somewhere?"

"Yes, of course. I'll be back as soon as that damn thing is over." At the door he kissed her. It was a longer, more complicated kiss than he had planned, and he cursed the need to hurry away. "Wait for me. I'll be right back."

The taxi, as he feared, took its time in arriving. The incessant rain, which hadn't let up for a minute all day, didn't help his clothes. In the rear seat, as the cab headed for the East Side, he discovered that his eyelids were heavy, that he felt a profound need to snatch a little sleep.

Were his words slurring, as he feared they had when he'd given the driver the address? Quietly, he recited his name aloud. "Mary had a little lamb, its fleece was white as snow," he added. It sounded okay, but he couldn't be sure.

"If you see a confectionary or candy store that's open, pull up, will you?" he called. That didn't sound too bad. No, it was fine. No one would suspect. The guesting job on the show wouldn't be too taxing, anyway, thank God, if he didn't want it to be. Danny Darrow, the professional barrel of monkeys who was RBS's comedy white hope, would be another one of the guests, and ardently loved nothing better than to filibuster a show's time with his gamut of built-in joke books. Bucky had pulled all the network wires to get Jim on this particular show—"Coast to coast exposure won't do anything but good for you," he'd counseled—and he wouldn't appreciate any personality slack. But the hell with it. The other rat racers had taught themselves to ease up and sprag. It was about time he learned the tricks, too.

At a luncheonette-newsstand, he hopped out, bought two uncapped bottles of Coca Cola and a Sunday *Times* and ran back to the waiting cab. Someone had told him that syrupy Coke could take the edge off a mild drunk far more quickly and effectively than coffee. He drank both as the taxi sped uptown, and hoped that his information had been right.

In the newspaper's television section he found the standard photograph of himself and the interview he'd given ten or twelve days ago. He was a little surprised to see that his quotes read so well; neither Evelyn nor Bucky had been able to be with him that afternoon, and he'd been afraid he'd bumbled the direct questions asked of him.

Bucky was stormily pacing back and forth when Jim hurried into his office.

"I called out the Marines, lookin' for you!" he cried. "I checked the hospitals and the gawddamn morgue! What the hell was this powder about? I thought you changed your gawddamn name from Creighton to Crater! What the hell're you tryin' to do, give me a coronary the hard way?"

"I'm here. Just calm down."

"Calm down, my bucket! Everybody in the country looks at this show except a couple of blind Eskimos! I had to stand on my head to get you a guest shot on it! Look'a what time it is!"

There was a change of clothes in the closet, fortunately. Jim stripped to his shorts and began to get into the fresh light blue shirt. "I got tied up, Bucky," he remarked, not fully ready to face him.

"Tied up? What the hell ties you up for a whole day? Where were you all day?"

"What's the difference where I was?" Jim snapped, aware of the cobwebs again, aware of the cumbrously heavy eyelids and the desperate urge to rest. "I'm here. I've never missed the clock yet. I thought you knew that."

"And what gives with Monica Enders, all of a sudden? She calls me up today and her voice is from eighty below. You were supposed to visit her last night on business and you didn't show. Monica *Enders*, for God's sweet sake! What were you doin', shacking up with some quiff you found?"

"I'm telling you just one more time, Bucky. You lay off. How I spend my few free minutes a day is my own concern … not your's, not Enders', not anybody's."

"But Enders … !"

"That's not your concern, either. Enders wanted to talk business with me last night like you wanted to do a fan-dance in Times Square. A hot time in the old town was the business she was interested in. This may disillusion you, but I'm not yet ready to be a male whore for Stander-Creighton Enterprises. Now can we drop it?"

Jim padded to his private washroom and decided that his eyes looked like a Rand-McNally road map and that Bruce, the makeup man, would have more than the usual amount of work for this show. Plugging his electric razor into the wall outlet, he wondered what was taking Bucky so long to get around to notice the rest of it.

"The next thing we do is get you some peppermint," Bucky advised, a bit less volcanically. "You smell like you lost your way in the Seagram Building."

"There's no smellovision yet."

"Do you know something I've just decided over the past couple of days? I knew when we dreamed up the *Hot Spot* format that it would be only a matter of time before the cockiness set in, that before long you'd discover not only that you invented the wheel, but that you created the heaven and the earth, too. But I sure as hell didn't think it'd happen so fast. You honest to God think you walk on water, don't you?"

The accusation hurt. "That's the last thing I think, Bucky," Jim said. "I'm sorry you don't know that."

"Maybe it's been my fault that I've spared you the grandpappy advice. Maybe I should've started pasting your ears back for you at the beginning of the game. You think I ride you, don't you, kid? You think I'm old Legree, out to milk every last ounce of profit there is in this roller-coaster."

"That does sum it up pretty well."

"Well, it's true," nodded Bucky. "We both have a good tennis match going here, and if I don't know anything else, I do know that one false step in this dog-eat-dog business can blow the dam." He stepped aside as Jim set down the razor and returned to the office to continue dressing. "I talk like I talk because I know more than you know. I've been in this radio game since the first days of The Happiness Boys and Joe Cook, and I was the first guy to know that TV could sell more than puppet shows and lessons on how to bake an upside-down cake. I've made a living in this racket because I haven't stopped for a minute to tie my shoelaces or kiss my wife. I've known that you never let the guard down, that the instant you do, there's thirty thousand other boys, just as studious, ready to take over. I've seen a warehouse full of world beaters who thought they could go to sleep under the money tree, that they were God's chosen gift. And today they're selling tickets to wrestling matches."

"I'm not buying any of that, Bucky," Jim maintained, reservedly at first. "I don't want to hear any more of the Godfrey humility speech because none of it applies to me. I'm *tired*, that's all. Can't you get that through that cash register of a brain? I'm bone tired, and so you think I'm getting out of line once in a while."

"You're a babe in the woods in this business. You're not forty yet! What do you have to be tired about? I still land on my feet after all these years because I decided never to let myself get tired!"

"What do I have to do with you?" Jim said. "I'm tired because for the past five months I've never rolled out of the bed once refreshed. For five months I've been scared to death that someone's going to come from around the corridor and find out that I don't belong where I am, that my place is back at the news-desk, letting the Gus Pattersons make the decisions. I spend ten, fifteen minutes a night before the show begins, calming the guests, and all the time I'm wondering if *I'll* have the guts to go on. Am I getting through to you, Bucky? It's strain, sweaty old-fashioned strain, and I feel a crackup coming. I feel like I'll never reach Labor Day. I like the nice suits and the waiters who know my name and the thirty-dollar shirts and the million shimmering women who want to lay me. And all of it's busting my head open because I'm scared!"

The telephone rang. Mr. Creighton was wanted in Studio 37. "Yeah" Bucky said, "He'll be right there."

"So now you know," Jim ventured gravely.

"All right, maybe you could've given you and me both a break and come to me sooner," Bucky observed at the door, not pressing so hard now. "Maybe we can still do something to—you know—pep you up, give you a little more spunk."

"Sure, sure," Jim nodded, heading for the elevator. "A pep-up pill is just what I need."

CHAPTER TWELVE

T HE THIRTY MINUTES of *Butcher, Baker* were an almost unen-
durably long thirty minutes for Jim Creighton, although he
knew shortly after the first commercial that he would swing it
without disaster.

Danny Darrow, as guaranteed, glibly interrupted everyone
and scattered his buckshot of one-line gags for a solid half of the
show. Jim spoke rarely—certainly never unless he was directly
expected to speak—and gave his turns at the mike quiet authority. The M.C., Mike Everett, told him privately afterwards that he
had served as the perfect counterbalance for Darrow, had been
the most prominent member of the panel because he had made
the least effort to be "on," and that he, Everett, would see the
agency tomorrow morning about a repeat invitation in another
few weeks.

Jim took the elevator back to his office, removed his
jacket, and had to peel the shirt from his chest and shoulders.
He tried to recall the last time stark fear had soaked him to
the skin.

The thought of entertaining Bucky again sickened him and
he locked his office door from the inside. He puttered with the
coffee percolator for a while and then set it back down; these
were the jitters, the abject jitters, and a cup of coffee wasn't going
to quell them. Dourly he went through a few of his desk draw-
ers in search of a tranquillizer, but dismissed that idea, too.
Tranquillizers took too damned long to start functioning, and

his nerves were pulled so taut that he couldn't hold still for longer than an instant at a time. He brought back the accordion door of the portable bar and picked up the nearest bottle to his hand, the twenty year old brandy that Evelyn had given him for his birthday.

Evelyn, he thought as he poured three inches into a glass and tossed them down his throat. *I promised to call her over the weekend, didn't I? It was Evelyn, wasn't it? No. Fran. Yes, I said I'd phone her on Sunday night.*

And Monica. If I have a grain of sense left in me, I'll at least telephone her. Oh baby, but I'm bushed. Oh brother, but how sweet it would be to crawl into a cave and just conk out for a month or two. Nuts. What good would that do? I'd have to wake up, wouldn't I? Cheers!

The first brandy magically removed some of the edge and magically took away the sweating. The second one didn't wholly pare the clinging anxieties but did relax his body. He carried the glass and the bottle to the swivel chair and, taking a deep breath, phoned Fran.

She and the Fraziers had seen him on TV and agreed that he'd come across wonderfully well. Yes, she was enjoying herself; she and Madge had played bridge all afternoon because of the rain and, would you ever believe it, Madge had lost a dollar and a quarter, and Madge was the world's champion bridge player! He'd looked a little tired on the screen; was he getting enough to eat? Getting enough sleep? Was Mrs. Wentsmann behaving herself? Yes, yes, yes, everything was all right, and how was she feeling? He hated himself for not summoning up more than what amounted to monosyllables, but he had never successfully talked with Fran on the telephone, and it seemed to command more strength that he had now to fill in the obvious gaps.

He told her to take care of herself, that he'd definitely find a way to get out to Cabott Island sometime next weekend, and that he'd better go now and look over some work before turning in.

"I understand, Jim, dear. Good night now."

The old man had pulled the same rotten stunts all the time, he thought ruefully now as he leaned back and poked around in the desk's side drawer for a cigarette.

Old Rudolph Valentino Creighton. Warren Gamaliel Harding Creighton, the prize stud of Western Pennsylvania. The handsome, clear-eyed, carnation-in-the-lapel fop, who had scintillating and seductive words for every woman in Haylesburg except his own wife. Jim would be in the house with her at dinnertime, and when the phone rang—if it rang at all—he knew what was to come next. "I'm tied up with this pesky inventory, Dorothea," he would sigh appealingly, "and I just don't know when I can get home. Better have supper without me."

Or: "You remember Bill Rooke, honey, he's our buyer. He's going to New York tomorrow morning to buy shoes, and he wants to go over things with me. You understand."

Or (when ritualistically-propped by liquor): "Be a good kid, kid, and find yourself a new playmate. I'm in love with a girl like never before in my whole life, and we need to be together. She's not a frigid hunk of ice like you. She's what can make a man go places and do things and make him feel like he's worth something."

"If he has so little regard for you," Jim asked his weeping mother, because he'd never had the guts to ask his father anything personal, "why doesn't he ask you for a divorce?"

"Stop, Jimmy …"

"Or why don't you ask him for one? Gosh, he thinks he's going to be young forever. He never really provides for you, and he gets stuck on every dam dame he sees. I've told you a million times. Why don't you just leave him? You know I'd take care of you. We'd leave this crummy town and I'd find a job somewhere ... Mr. Weaver says I have a good speaking voice and he has all these contacts with big radio people in New York City ... and I'd look out for you. Maybe you'd even meet somebody nice in New York City that would really appreciate you."

"You're so good, Jimmy. I can't leave him. He has That Old Craziness now, but when he wakes up he'll be bright as a button. You wait and see. You're too young to understand, I guess, but he needs me. You can't leave anybody if they need you. You have to remember that always."

She died less than a month after Jim arrived by bus in New York. The old man, his shoulder completely healed from the bullet wound, had lost his section manager's job at The Vanity, and the service clubs of Haylesburg advised him, in one way or another, that his days as a joiner were over, but he did land a salaried job as clerk at Leiken's Shoe Mart on Gilbert Avenue. He promised Mother that his silly days were over, and that from here on in he would make her proud of him.

On the first Saturday night, he waited until all the customers and other clerks had left the store and confronted Sol Leiken in the office. He knocked Leiken unconscious, stole the day's receipts, and was never heard from again.

The police reported the news to Mother. The neighbors on Arbutus Street were under the impression that she accepted the news bravely, perhaps a little too bravely. An hour later she suffered a heart attack, and ten days later Jim and Harry, back from New York, buried her....

How is it supposed to fit in? Jim Creighton wondered now in the plush WRBS office, as he had wondered again and again from the moment he had learned that he had the makings of a television personality and automatically was expected to raise his head out of the sand. *I don't know if that man who was my father is alive or dead, but I'll hate him for his weakness and cruelty until the day I die.*

I loathe everything connected with him. And I am doing everything in my power to be exactly like him.

Almost as if he had cued himself, he sat forward, filled his emptied brandy glass, and dialed Ginny's number.

"Hello?" she exclaimed, as though she had momentarily lost her breath in racing to the phone.

"This is The Creighton Video Survey, madam," Jim intoned, hastily feeling on safe ground again. "Sorry to get you out of your bath. Would you kindly tell us what video program you were viewing this evening?"

"Say, was I ever t'rilled wit' delight, like!" she affirmed, immediately falling into character. "Like, I watched duh Roller Doiby clear troo, an' it was like a gawjuss gasser, like!"

"You bitch," he laughed.

"Darling," Ginny enthused, "it's remarkable. You were miraculous! You took the play away from everyone! I couldn't have been more happy for you."

"It wasn't easy, Mom."

"I'm sure it wasn't. Where are you now? Still drenched from this ghastly rain, I'm sure."

"As a matter of fact, I'm sitting in my office, snifting a twenty-year-old brandy in my undershorts. And I'm commencing to feel fairly content with myself."

"You pompous old fool," Ginny snickered. "I can just see you, swirling that swivel chair from left to right to left again. Before you know it, you'll say, 'Now where in tarnation are my glasses?' and your twenty-two grandchildren will clap their hands and yelp, 'They're on your forehead, you old poop!' "

"That's enough out of you, whippersnapper. It so happens they *are* on my forehead. Tarnation!"

"When will you be down here so I can say more and more and more about how gorgeous you were on that gruesome show?"

"Very soon. Half an hour. I feel like eating something exotic, like lox and bagels. Where can I buy some?"

"At The Tid-Bit Shop, on Houston Street," Ginny said. "No, forget it. It'll take you too long. I'll run out now while you're looking for a taxi and find some lox and bagels. It may all look like sturgeon and protein bread, but it'll be lox and bagels. A deal?"

"That's my girl," Jim said and wished some silver button could be pressed to get him there and in her arms in the very next breath.

Rousing himself to change to the rumpled but not dry clothes he had brought to this studio, he thought tentatively of what might conceivably bubble into tension in this office tomorrow morning, when the new week would officially begin. *How do you let on that you're prepared for business as usual to sagacious observers such as Bucky Stander, when Ginny Grant is in the vicinity and your happiness is glowing through your skin? And how do you effectually hide what you feel for Ginny Grant when you have a sharp eagle eye like Evelyn Shoreham on board?*

Those quibbles would present themselves tomorrow, Jim thought resignedly as he finished his good brandy, scooped up the cigarette ashes methodically, and switched off the lights. He tipped a dollar to Emile, the doorman who brought a taxi from out of nowhere with a snap of the fingers and, settling in the back seat, noticed that he had carried the brandy bottle in his jacket pocket all the way to the cab.

Chuckling, he uncorked it and tipped it to his lips. *Here's to you, Evelyn,* he toasted. *You're great. You're the incompetent's best friend. You're The Coliseum! The Louvre Museum! You're Mickey Mouse!*

CHAPTER THIRTEEN

E VELYN SHOREHAM WALKED through her compact five-room apartment, chain-smoking, and knew finally that it was time for the warm milk and third nembutal. She had always detested anything artificial, even artificial ways to get to sleep, but she could't afford another tossing night. The sleeping pill trick hadn't failed very often.

Once, years ago, before she had left Waco to sniff for those pieces of gold in the Manhattan streets, Paul Arden had asked her to marry him. His father was the city's leading attorney, and a wedding with Paul would have meant a big house, and maids, and clean bed linens every night. Paul hadn't done more than kiss her once, and then he'd proposed.

Her parents had urged her to accept the offer, but Evelyn had found a way to turn him down without making him lose Waco face. She had a career ahead of her in New York. She sensed it, she felt it, and marriage would only stop her from realizing how big she could be.

There had been one affair, with a counterman from Bickford's Cafeteria, a freckled boy named Kenny, who had been a neighbor in Waco and who wanted to go on the stage. She had exalted in calling herself his mistress (he had brought all his shaving equipment and his T-shirts to her room on Columbus Avenue), and for more than an active month, while she had made the rounds of the important radio stations and had landed a job at Rockland, had somehow found the money to bring him cigarettes and newspapers. She had known, even during the most accommodating moments, that he was beneath her and would eventually have to go. Once she knew her job was secure and that she would never again have to beg for help, she booted him out. She never thought of him again for more than moments at a time.

She met other men, of course, as her career developed. A raft of married men, a sprinkling of predestined bachelors, and even two or three men who wanted to marry her. She slept with those she thought could best help her advance in a cutthroat business. When she came to the devastating conclusion that doing this made no perceptible difference in the way she was advancing, she cut it out.

The rain had let up, thank Heaven, she thought as she slipped into her double bed and wondered why that third pill wasn't making her drowsy. Twice before, during the truly hectic times at the studio, she'd swallowed a fourth; three would have been enough, she knew, if she'd given them a chance to go to work, and she'd felt traitorously guilty for days after for defying Dr. Rooney's strict order against even two. Tomorrow, Monday, would begin the normal corker of a week, and she desperately needed a sound night's sleep.

What the hell? A fourth hadn't killed her yet. Sighingly, she reached into her night-table drawer and popped the tablet into her mouth. She lighted a cigarette, forgetting that she hadn't put out the one before, and dropped the match in the general direction of the tray.

Tomorrow morning she would have to go after Jim, face to face, and, arranging her words so that no balance would be lost, again apologize for behaving like some Bowery Follies harpie. He was soft and oh so malleable, particularly when anything representing authority approached him, and he would say something forgiving like, "I've already forgotten it." Still, she would have to make sure the case would be unalterably closed; she had made the industry's single cardinal mistake of having momentarily lost control of herself, and it would have to be rectified.

"Why are you such a driving woman, Evelyn?" asked Greg Horrigan, mercilessly chiding her.

The voice was uninvited and abrupt and her eyes opened in alarm. No. She was alone in her own comfortable five-room apartment. One of those hypnagogic dreams, the calling up of a hurtful recollection just a moment before you go to sleep. Gregory Horrigan, that playboy vice-president from Imperial Broadcasting, had been the first confirmed bachelor she had thought would pull all the expedient wires for her. She had given herself to him, detesting him for playing emotional Halloween, and he had mocked her through that bitter weekend, telling her she was too driving, too teeth-clenchingly ambitious to ever be of any real use to anyone else or to herself.

A dream, she told herself. *Hallucination stuff. Dime a dozen, pampered theatrics.*

The kaleidoscope of the past sloughed past her as she both welcomed sleep and struggled to fight it off. The impeccably-barbered Radio City men who invited her to their apartments and never neglected to advise her she was sparring a losing battle against a man's world. The superiors to whom she had to stand ground. The inferiors who thought they knew more about mass communications than she did. The office parties where the pompadoured office boys felt free to pinch every woman in the studio except Miss Shoreham. One of the married men from one of the top networks who asked her, much too bloated with sympathy, "Why can't you unfreeze, Evelyn? Your instincts are so good. What's wrong with being a woman?"

Everything became splendidly vivid as she felt herself drifting off to sleep. The sight of her mother and father playing a duet of *Down Among the Sheltering Palms* at the piano. The smell of the smoking leaves from Mr. Ramsay's front yard next door in Waco. The sight of Billy Kunstler, the doctor's boy, coming up on the porch and selling his father's anti-vivisectionist tracts for three cents a copy. The smell of smoke. The smell of smoke. The smell …

I can't get up.

I smell smoke, and I'm scared, and that table's on fire, and I don't have the strength to get up and put it out.

"Strength, Evelyn," one of those barbared men had grinned at her. "Why do you have to keep proving you have more muscles than men have?"

God, save me. The whole wall seems to be on fire. I can make it. I can get up. Drowsy. Oh Lord, don't let me go to sleep. I put the cigarette out, didn't I?

"I'm here, Evelyn," *Jim had said. Poor Jim Creighton. You're too weak to last in this man's army. You belong back on the farm, smoking a corn cob pipe and raking leaves with Mr. Ramsay. If I should die before I wake. O Loving God in the sky, what's happening? I'm chained to this bed, I can't save myself.*

"Keep up with your joking," she told Greg Horrigan, "but I'm going to carry radio and television around in my pocket some day."

"Best wishes and a Happy New Year," Greg Horrigan laughed.

"Thanks," said Evelyn Shoreham, minutes before she burned to death.

Bucklin Stander drove home to his duplex apartment on Central Park South, wishing that he could have avoided that second-act-curtain scene with Jim.

It could have waited till tomorrow, or till next week. Sure, he'd seen the change in Creighton—if they changed, they changed all of a sudden, the way this one did—but he hadn't had to shoot off his mouth that way. Enough was going on. His wife was talking about changing psychoanalysts again, which was a far more vital topic around her part of Manhattan than was the possibility of a bomb dropping over the Paramount. His older daughter was about to give birth to his first grandchild at Harkness Pavillion. His younger daughter was failing in her grades at Bennington because, she kept writing, he made her feel left out with an allowance of only $100 a week. How could she hold her head up?

He was tired, and knew it, recognized it. He would be fifty-six in September and he felt twice as old by this time of night. Everything was riding on Creighton—his nurturing over the months, his plans, his hopes to keep the big money motor running—and Creighton was going to fold like a cardboard house unless he used his brain in a hurry. The trouble was that he wasn't nearly so quick on the trigger as he had been a few years ago.

The long talk with the boy had meant found-money, late last year. Creighton had been one of Gus Patterson's pets and had been shoved into every important news coverage on RBS-TV. "This kid can become Santa Claus with the right handling," Patterson had confided over a drink at Shor's. "He looks like Cary Grant, his face and voice are sincerity itself, and he has that vanishing quality of making a viewer or listener think that he believes every word he says, whether he's talking about thermo-dynamics or Ex-Lax. He's no deep thinker, but he knows how to ask direct questions and then juggle the answers with all the charm of a sleepy Little Boy Blue. You're crazy if you don't goose him into a fast contract, Stander. If he's worked right, the public will buy Confederate dimes from him."

Patterson was right. There had been the fifteen-dollar dinner at The Harwyn, with just enough and not too many drinks, and the boy had said Yes, there *were* a couple of ideas he'd been kicking around. What about an interview show on television that would depart from the tired press releases and ask questions everyone in the living room would like to ask? An interview show with real meat. And at a late hour, when the Berle and Welk and Godfrey viewers would be safely tucked away in bed?

"Sounds like you got something, Jim," Bucky had nodded. "Let's put it on at Keokuk and see how it gets off the helicopter."

The show, *Jim Creighton's Hot Spot*, was slipped into the channel slot as furtively as a satyr at YWCA. It clicked. Creighton knew his way around *a priori* research and was able to startle the potato-chip munchers with his seemingly off-the-cuff knowledge of maritime law, cloture procedure, and Hollywood intrigues. With no concerted inducements the mail began to pour in. Dozens, then scores, then hundreds. They liked this Jim Creighton. The stay-up-late New Yorkers believed that handsome Jim Creighton asked the stuffed shirts the questions they would liked to have asked, and was neither smarter nor dumber than his audience.

This gold mine started to build, Bucky recalled. He looked like Cary Grant, like Patterson said. *I'm supposed to be a shrewdie. Why didn't I take a minute to find out for sure if he could weather the big deal storms? Now he tells me he's ready to cave, and maybe he even looks it, and I have every fish in my barrel banked on him.*

I made him. I made him as sure as Ford made cars. He's getting the jeebies, and it's up to me to see that he doesn't turn into Jello. If he folds up, how many more chances do I have?

Ziggie the doorman relieved him of the Lincoln and told him that his wife had come home an hour ago. He thanked him, rode upstairs, and came upon his wife mixing a Martini.

"You look like somebody just stole your pocket book" Bucky charged. "What's the matter?"

"Haven't you heard? Evelyn Shoreham. The studio just called. She's dead."

"Evelyn's dead! ... How?"

"All they know so far is that she fell asleep and left a cigarette burning. The bedroom went up in flames. What could be more unnerving? I tried to get my analyst for an emergency session, but he hasn't come back yet from Cape Cod. Oh, everything's so dreadful!"

Bucky staggered for a moment and then demanded, "Get me Jim's home number."

"What, dear?" his wife asked absently, completing a monumental Martini.

"Jim Creighton's home phone. Get it for me."

"Do you know I've been trying to get through to Dr. Abbott all day long?" his wife said, raising the drink to her wrinkled lips. In 1925, when he'd met her, she had been waiting tables at a fish house on Staten Island. "He told me that the dream I had—you know, the one I told you about—about the tall, thin man who sold bananas to lines of ovals was the best dream I'd ever had and I should keep thinking about it? Well, I've applied it to ..."

"Just go to hell, will you?" he barked.

"Bucklin!"

"And take your mind-reader along with you. Evelyn's dead! I liked her, and I want you to help me find Jim Creighton so we can tell him, if he doesn't know."

"Will you get it through your head that Dr. Abbott says that an undue reaction to death ..."

"You are going to get on that phone and try to find Jim for me," Bucky said, "or I'm going to break every brittle bone in your body. Do you hear me?"

He looked for a cigar in his mammoth apartment as his wife scurried out of the room. The meaning of the corporation would change. The meaning would be different. The woman who had known how to knit everything together, to keep an aging shipwreck like Bucky Stander and a young dummy like Jim Creighton afloat, was gone. The calls to the fancy employment agencies would be made tomorrow for a replacement, first thing. And they wouldn't turn up a shadow of Evelyn Shoreham.

The future, somehow, relied entirely on Bucky Stander.

"You look tired around the eyes, much too tired to join me in duh Roller Doiby," said Ginny Grant as he returned to her apartment. "You need a week's sleep."

"Make it two weeks and I'm with you," he nodded, kissing her and only incidentally remembering to ask if she'd come up with the lox and bagels.

"They're ready and waiting," she informed. "But maybe you'd better have a drink first to loosen up the raveled sleeve of care. I see you carry your own," she added, relieving him of Evelyn's brandy.

"Maybe," Jim replied dutifully. "All I want at this point is Ovaltine and a tin whistle, but maybe you're right."

"There aren't too many man-sized drinks left in it, but I have an extra supply. Get in bed, take off your shoes, say a few mumbling words about how much you appreciate my loving you, and I'll bling you native gull's magic elixir."

He listless picked at his food as Ginny put on the warming Gerry Mulligan records, and decided that he had no special interest in any more hooch. He said so. She made no issue of it, but made him a stiff one a few minutes later. Smiling, Jim agreed that no one in his right mind ever purposely forgoes an already-built drink.

Ginny made herself more than generously responsive to him after they had switched off the lights, and this revived and delighted him. He was very drunk, he suspected, slurringly and perhaps boringly drunk, and kept reminding her that the alarm would ab-sho-lutely have to be set at a minute before five. The next thing he remembered was that she brought him a bullshot and hot coffee, greeted, "Good morning, darling," and tuned in to Chet Mitchell's show. They both sat up in the narrow bed, sipping their morning coffee like two comfortable married folks. Jim nuzzled at her ear and had begun to tell her again how much she meant to him, when Chet announced that Evelyn Shoreham had perished last night in a fire.

His cup dropped. The coffee scalded his leg. He was too overcome to cry out.

CHAPTER FOURTEEN

B UCKY WAS IN HIS, Jim's, office when Jim entered it at a quarter of seven. They nodded solemnly to one another and for several minutes neither spoke.

"I asked Mitchell to take over your news shows today," Bucky said finally, his voice heavy and strained, "and he said he'll be glad to. I didn't think you'd much want to do it."

"That was thoughtful, Buck. Thanks." Then: "Where is she now?"

"At Westbrook. So far as anybody can find out she doesn't have a relative in the world."

"I'll pick up the tab for the funeral."

"Aw, nobody's gonna expect that, Jim ..."

"I know that. I said I want to pay for it. Now tell me what happened. Does anyone have the whole story yet?"

Bucky appeared to know little more than had been said on the radio. They both talked about Evelyn, haltingly and with kindled emotion that couldn't successfully be contained, and soon Jim walked unsteadily to his bathroom and was sick.

"Will there be a show tonight?" he asked flatly as he returned.

"Why not?" Bucky asked, as though the question were mildly ridiculous. "We're still in business, aren't we?"

"Who's the guest? I can't seem to focus."

"Rufus Neall, the former middleweight who just became a minister."

"Oh. Yeah."

"The first thing I did was to look over Evelyn's file on him in her office. Thank God it's as complete as it is. Oh, and I've put out some feelers-already about tracking down Rose Crawford to take over. The right kind of money talk'll get her over here. She's been working for Barry Coles, but his Trendex is way off and there're noises that his sponsor's gonna dump him.

Jim blinked at him. "Rose Crawford? That's a little soon, isn't it?"

"Soon? What should we wait for, Christmas? Losing Evelyn is like a hefty kick in *my* belly, too. but we have to keep the wheels rolling, don't we?"

"Um. I guess you're right."

Alone, he found that the persistent feeling of guilt would not go away. On the phone she had made that pitifully upbeat plea for him to come to her, and he had promptly forgotten her.

Ginny looked in on him anxiously at half past seven, more than an hour earlier than she was expected to arrive. "Okay to come in?" she inquired solicitously. He nodded and she closed the door after her. She had been remarkably stirred by the news report, too, and had striven to comfort his grief with what at the time hadn't seemed at all to be a motherly embrace. Now she moved quietly to the unplugged coffee pot and lifted it. "Nobody's made any coffee for you," she said. "Or is coffee mollycoddle stuff now? You look as if you'd do better with a drink or two under your belt."

His face felt granular, his body leaden. Why was she always so eager to open the jug for him, to keep him in a state close to unconsciousness? "Coffee," he replied. "Coffee will taste good now."

"A little slug in the coffee, then," she recommended, heading for the bar. "It's been such a shocking experience that ..."

"Damn it, I said coffee!" he snapped, impatient with her for the first time, impatient with her overbearing passion to be so constantly supportive.

She retreated a step and regarded him as though he had struck her, and then nodded understandingly. "You're right, darling. I don't mean to keep on your neck. Coffee coming up." She came to him as she waited for it to perc and kissed his forehead. Automatically his hand raised and touched her arm. "I know how important she was. I'll try to stay scarce today and be of as much help as I can, both at the same time."

Jim's eyes followed her as she returned to the coffee pot, as she obviously attempted to pry his thoughts from Evelyn for wisps of time. "I saw Bucky on the way up here" (*Bucky?* he repeated to himself; *since when does Bucky have a first name for her?*) "and he was shaken up, too. Naturally. He said you wouldn't do any news today but that you would do *Hot Spot.* I told him I'd do anything with the Rufus Neall story that you or he wanted. I even have a peck of ideas to lighten your load a bit tonight during the program."

"Not now, Ginny …"

"Of course, dearest. I didn't mean that. Later on in the day. If you like, if I have permission I'll see his manager, Ned Travis, and see what we can come up with. Travis is supposed to be a very intelligent, astute man."

"Anything, Ginny."

"Yes, of course. There I go again. This coffee will be ready in a minute and then I'll get out of your way."

Before she left, Ginny kissed him again, gently, shieldingly, and crooked her forefinger under his chin so that he would have to look up at her. "Try to rest as much as you can, darling," she urged. "The next week or so will be hell for you, but you won't be alone. Perhaps it's a little mad to say this, after we've known one another for only a few days, but I love you terribly. I love you more deeply than any woman has ever loved you, and I want to take care of you. For as long as you'll let me."

She went out of the office, as gracefully as she had come in.

The late morning and early afternoon papers were delivered to him and he noticed, as he tiredly leafed through them, that all of them carried the story of the fire and that two of the afternoon columnists mentioned her passing with genuine regret. Herb Graham, Clif, Juggy, the engineer, Peg Robbins, and even Pinky, the copy boy, stopped in to share their sadness with him. He received them all, and knew eventually that it was time for him to go downtown to see her.

At the undertaking parlor, a dapper, black-suited man with ice-cold eyes that suggested he mourned professionally, had been alerted that Jim would pay the bill. "Begging your pardon, sir," he intoned, "but I strongly recommended that the coffin be closed throughout. The unfortunate deceased's face was burned almost beyond recognition. There was very little we could do."

"I wanted to see her."

"Believe me, sir, it's better this way."

"Yes. Very well. Will you take me to the coffin?"

He stood alone before the narrow, somehow extraordinarily long box as the canned music was being piped into the room from some celestial corner, and stared half dazedly. *You called out to me, Evelyn*, he said silently. *You came to me for help and I was too busy weeping over my own ineffectual, screwed up life to hear you. I apologize. I apologize for giving nothing.*

There was a faint sound of someone approaching from behind him, and he stood erect. A small, sparsely built, expensively dressed man of perhaps fifty then stood beside him, nodded to him as if the two knew each other, and crossed himself.

A tenuous moment elapsed before the man, vaguely familiar, smiled wanly.

"I haven't seen Evelyn for I guess nearly eight years. But I always felt if I needed a favor, she'd drop everything to come to me."

"You're Al Gallagher," Jim remembered, and abruptly recalled Walley Brunow's linking him with Moran and Spector as men who had known Ginny Grant.

"That's right, Jim. We met a few times at Toots Shor's bar and once at The 500 Club in Atlantic City. If you think you're up to it now, I'll buy us a drink at The Algonquin. It's only a block or so away."

They both ordered Scotch, and Gallagher finished his in a half dozen swift gulps. "Death," he grinned, facing Jim. "I've lost nine-tenths of the people who mean anything to me, and I still can't get used to looking at caskets." He asked for another, a double, and grinned again. "I used to think when I was a kid in Tacoma that when I reached my fifties, nothing would scare me. That shows you what kind of masterminds we raise in Tacoma. The older I get, the more of a sissy I become. You're not drinking, Jim."

"That was nice of you, Al, paying your respects to Evelyn," Jim said, liking him.

"I was fond of Evelyn," Gallagher nodded. "I know how all the backbiters and hungry clowns in television called her driving and too ambitious. Sure she was. What was she supposed to do in this mad-doctor industry, simper in a corner and suck her thumb? Sure, she wasn't a Bardot or a Betty Boop; I don't think she had any more sex in her than that taxidermist we met back at The Westbrook. But when she competed in a man's business, it was never as a man—it was always on the up and up, a worker who knew her stuff. I'm right, right? She worked for you and Stander. You must have seen that she never put on a vest and Army shoes."

Jim nodded. "Yes, you're right. She was strictly business, from our equivalent of nine to five. None of us ever really remembered she had a gender."

"Exactly."

"But maybe she thought about it, after she got home at night."

"Sure, I'm certain she did," Gallagher agreed. "But within her work day she performed one hell of a function, no matter where she was employed, and she allowed for no hokey nonsense. She was the last of the red-hot genderless workers in our field. Not like the wolfess pack of dynamos that usually crop up. The thumb suckers who suddenly learn and want to take over. Shrikes. Scorpions. Dragon Ladies. The antenna's full of 'em."

"Could be I'm losing you," Jim said guardedly. "I haven't come up across any lady scorpions."

Gallagher chuckled. "Then your incredible luck's holding out. By damn, I remember one scorpion! She was shorter than even me, and I'm two feet-five, but she had a shape on her and a brilliant way of swinging it around that made men flip their executive lids. We hired her over at my factory as an assistant researcher, and before I could turn around she's Albert Einstein with a 36-B cup. Before I knew it, like the comic books say, she made a dash for me—subtly, you understand, ever so subtly—and made me think I was Rock Hudson. And you may have gathered by now that I'm not Rock Hudson. She was trying to get me to drop the bulk of my staff and put her in charge. No background, no real preparation for the job—just an itch to rule the man's roost and then leave him for dead." Gallagher blinked at his second Scotch and impulsively drained it. "Like with Finnegan. I knew she'd cozied up to Finnegan at Monarch and he'd knocked himself off after a couple of concerted weeks."

"She was Asa Finnegan's girl?" Jim asked, playing dumb.

"Oh, brother, was she?" Gallagher smirked. "The point is, I knew she'd gone to work at Monarch with something like the status of a dishwasher, and all of a sudden was Finnegan's home away from home. It was all sub rosa info, and who can nail down sub rosa facts in our TV garden of verses? But the fact is I knew she was indirectly responsible for old Asa's committing suicide, and I hired her, anyway. Just call me Boob McNutt."

"Responsible? How? Who was she? What was her name?"

Restlessly waiting for his third drink, Gallagher laughed aloud. "Oh, no, tales I never tell out of school. Ginny thought she could own and operate Imperial Broadcasting just a week after she went to work for it, and she played me for a prize sucker, telling me I was the greatest thing since bubble gum, and finally I had to get rid of her. But name her? Mister, that would make me something in the nature of a cad, no?"

It took time and several more drinks to wheedle the rest out of him. And even if the rest was made of lies and boys'-school exaggerations, as Jim prayed it was, there still was Asa Finnegan, the mild, well-meaning, incompetent old man whose father had given him the reins of a huge industry he hadn't been remotely equipped to handle. Scores of people had been brought in to do the work and make the decisions, while Old Asa got progressively drunker and showed up now and then at industry dinners to proudly accept plaques for having contributed so much to mass communications. Everyone in radio and TV knew how hopeless he was, and everyone pitied him. There had been one last gasp of life, when he'd appeared to be trying to live up to the honorable legend, and then, the story went, he had taken up with a girl in his office. Although doctors warned him that the drinking was quickly wrecking his liver, something about his association with the girl, evidently accelerated the drinking, accelerated his swift, artless suicide.

Ginny? Jim thought. *My Ginny?*

"You say that this girl was a scorpion," Jim remarked. "But she didn't destroy you, did she? Or any of the other men in the business? And did she actually cast a supernatural hex on Finnegan?"

"No, of course not," Gallagher laughed. "The reason most of us got out from under without getting scorched was that we weren't ready to be cracked open. Finnegan was. Weak, scared, wide open for the kill. No, no man can be sent to hell if he doesn't want to be. It's only when he can't walk on his own two legs that a scorpion takes over and gives him the final whammy."

The man set his glass down and refused to let Jim pay the check. "Well, back to the coal mines. Be nice to have a drink with you again, Jim. Under happier circumstances, of course."

When he returned to his office, Jim found a note in Peg Robbins' sturdy backhand which read. "Ned Travis called twice. Please call back. OD 1-2190." The wall clock read 3:29 and *Disk Doctor* was playing the new Dinah Shore album.

Jim dialed the number of Rufus Neall's manager, and he turned out to be as obligingly helpful as Ginny had said. "I'm sorry to be bothering you, Mr. Creighton, I know you must be extremely busy," greeted Travis, who had seen young Neall through four or five middleweight championships and then had managed him through a rejection of boxing and an entrance into the ministry. "Rufus and I heard of that fine Miss Shoreham's death about noon today and we want to send our condolences."

"Thank you, Mr. Travis," said Jim. The man's voice was old, creaking, Kentuckian.

"It's hard to see how she could have been nicer or more encouraging to Rufus, especially when she saw how nervous he was about appearing on your program tonight. Your very charming vice-president was kind to him, too."

"My vice-president?"

"Mrs. Grant," said Travis. "She left here a few minutes ago. She agreed that it would be terribly hard to take Miss Shoreham's place in your organization, but I'm certain she'll be a credit to you."

Jim sat up.

"We'll be there on time, Mr. Creighton, rest assured. Ah— may I ask when the funeral services for Miss Shoreham will be? We'd like so much to attend, if that's all right."

"You certainly may, sir. It will probably be the day after tomorrow. We'll let you know."

So it's beginning. No time like the present. No time lost.

He glanced through The Dispatch and came across Steve Lobeck's column, Video, U.S.A. The lead item read: "What brass knuckle, knuckleheaded interviewer, who loves to put other people on the hot spot, regrets that he has but one wife to send to the country? Since she's been away, junior's been thumbing his long hawk nose at The 7th Commandment. Attention, knucklehead: cut it out pronto or this corner will glady print names and places that will turn the stomachs of decent N. Y. Televiewers and will put you back in the junkheap, where you and your Commie-loving pals belong."

Don't fight back, Bucky had advised. Maybe he'll go away.

Ginny was brighteyed and undeniably sure of herself when she returned to his office, carrying what probably was another neatly-typed stack of perceptive notes. "You're going to be ploud of native gull yet, darling," she pledged, placing the papers before him. "This stuff is awfully preliminary so far, but if you agree with some of this, you'll be able to coast through the show tonight without ..."

"I understand you're my new vice-president," Jim said.

She blinked. "Where did you hear that?"

"From Travis. Is it true? Is that how you identified yourself?"

"Oh, that," Ginny said, not quite laughing, rising to it. "Maybe you're right, maybe I should've minded my protocol. But most people are extremely impressed by titles—the way Travis and Neall were—and it certainly made the interview a lot easier to get."

The phone rang. Herb said, "Jim, do you think there's any chance of your doing the six o'clocker after all? Chet'll do it, he says, but he sure looks and sounds bushed. If you feel you're not up to it, of course ..."

"Sure, I'll do it. I'm okay now, Herb. There's no reason why I shouldn't."

"Great. Then can you hop right down so we can piece it together?"

"Yeah, I'll be right along."

"What was that, dear?" Ginny asked. "The six o'clock show? Can't they do anything by themselves? You know you're not up to broadcasting. The *Hot Spot* tonight will be rough enough on you, won't it?"

He felt muddled, oddly bewildered by his feelings as he rose. "Ginny, it may not have been brought to your attention, but when I fall down and go boom I don't automatically break. I'm a big boy now."

"You're angry with me."

"I think I am, yes. I haven't had enough time to think it all through."

Now she was worriedly advancing to him, again taking his arm. "Darling, I can understand everything. It's been a beastly day for you and you're tired and irritable. All I want to do is to help wherever I can. Yes, of course, I said I was more than a sixty-five-a-week lackey and I want to use my skills. Are those crimes? Until you've sorted out the mess here, I can do Evelyn's job perfectly well, and you know that as well as I."

"We'll talk about it."

"You know you need me, don't you, dearest? You need me because you love me. You know that with all respect to Evelyn, she was the great dictator here with you, she never gave you room to express yourself, to even breathe like a man. I can take care of you better than she did. She fought you all the way, thought she was better than you. You know that all I want for you is to see you strong and in command of your ..."

He faced her squarely. "Who was Asa Finnegan?" he asked.

The name was a blow that merely grazed her. She took a moment and then answered, "He was in charge of Monarch Broadcasting, wasn't he?"

"You worked for Monarch, didn't you? Wouldn't you know?"

"Yes, of course. I was confused for a second. Indirectly I did work for him, yes, for a very short period of time. I didn't like it there at all. Mossbacked old fuddies with ..."

"How long were you his mistress before he died?"

An anguish raised in her face and she slapped Jim's cheek. There was a frozen moment of anger, before she brought the hand to her mouth in pious horror.

"I'm sorry, darling," she exclaimed. "I didn't mean to do that!"

"Thanks," he said. "I have my answer." He opened the office door and stepped into the corridor. She followed him as far as she dared. When he reached the elevators he turned his head, but she wasn't anywhere to be seen.

When he got back at twenty past six, there was a sealed envelope on his desk. *Mr. Creighton* was written on it. The letter read:

> "My dearest darling, I would give my life if my ghastly hysterics could have been avoided. I didn't realize that E's death put me under some strain, too, although certainly not to the extent that I had any right to touch you in anger. You must believe me when I swear that the filthy gossip you heard is absolutely untrue, that there is a perfectly simple explanation, that I cannot live if you don't give me the chance to explain it to you. I will be at home, waiting for you after your show tonight. I beg you to come. I adore you. G."

Arnie came in to give him a massage. He had one contemplative bourbon, and then went out of the building for a private, leisurely dinner. Steve Lobeck was in the office, mixing himself a drink, when Jim came back.

"I thought the exterminator was in here this morning and got rid of the cockroaches," Jim objected quietly, surprised to find him here.

Lobeck laughed and peered at the Bell's he was generously pouring. He seemed a trifle high. "Great sense of humor, champ. I didn't think you'd mind. I'm taking most of the evening off from swimming the channels. I wrote a think-piece for tomorrow's paper."

"'Think'? You?" Jim stated. "I always imagined that was against the natural law." He lighted a cigarette and felt faintly queasy. "Look, I have a lot on my mind, Lobeck. Condense your noble admission of saintliness, speak your scummy piece, and then go play in traffic."

"I can take it," Lobeck shrugged indifferently and sidled with his drink to the armchair. "Keep it up. I might even get to like it. Once you hear what I've come for, though, I think you'll talk a little less snotty." He sat and comfortably crossed his legs. "I'm willing to call a truce, guy."

"A what?"

"See? You thought I'd never give in, didn't you? You'll learn I carry weight in this town, but that I don't abuse it unless I'm forced to."

Jim crossed the room and took his seat. "I'm listening."

"There's a lot I know about you, champ," Lobeck asserted blandly, "more than you think anybody knows. I got interested in you when you put that parade of Commies on your show after my friend "Whippy" Whipper was nice enough to let you rip him apart." Whipper, one of *Hot Spot*'s first guests, believed that Fascism was the answer to all of man's ills and was the coming thing in America. Jim had allowed him to return twice, and on three other occasions had invited other supporters to defend his cause.

"By Commies," said Jim, "You mean the man from The Republican National Committee, the man from the Mayor's office, and those women who'd worked for Taft's nomination."

"Still Commies. What's that prove?"

"Okay, so you put me under your microscope. So?"

"So a couple of my friends were only too happy to dig up some mighty interesting research on you. Item one, that you married your wife because you knocked her up. Item two, that you have no record of being a member of a church. Item three, that your father was a crook and a adulterer in some jerkwater town in Pennsylvania. Item four, that you have a little twist tucked away in the Village. We don't know who she is yet, but that won't take long to find out."

Jim regarded the friendly smile on the man's face. "Mind if I ask you something?"

"Shoot."

"How does human garbage like you approach a mirror? Can you honestly look at one without puking?"

Unperturbed, Lobeck grinned more widely. "Uh-uh. I told you to mind you manners, buster. To tell the truth, I can't figure you out. I never could. You could've made a friendly overture to me long ago and I could've helped you, but you were too proud, or something. Even now, when you know I can go home and play my typewriter and when the sheet's pulled out you'll be washed up—not only on local TV but on that network deal that's set for fall—even now, you're insulting me. I'm the *press*, jack! Don't you know what can happen to you when I really decide to open fire?" He sat forward. "Freshen my drink a little?" he inquired placidly.

"You mentioned a truce," Jim stated. "If I do something for you, you'll drop all the charges. What's the favor?"

Lobeck snickered easily and sat back again. "Now we understand each other. You met that girl with me at Costello's, Mindy Spears. The one you insulted."

"I felt bad about that after I left. I called up all my friends at three in the morning and had them do research on her. They found out that if it hadn't been for the Negro-Catholic Plot, she would've been a famous surgeon today."

"Very funny. Save your gags for the funny papers. What I want is very simple, Creighton. I want you to have her on your show as soon as possible. I want you to banner her with announcements, beginning tonight, real Barnum ballyhoo, play her up big as the greatest songstress in the land. I want you to sell her every night till she appears. Then I'll have the copy written up. You can read your questions, she'll have memorized her answers. Simple, isn't it?"

Jim eyed him carefully. "You're really serious, aren't you?"

"Sure I am. I dig the little chick. You know what that feeling's about, don't you, champ? You'd put on a little more steam to sell a chick you liked, wouldn't you? Sure. So it's settled, check? You sell Mindy, and I give you my word that I'll tear up all the evidence I have against you and I'll even treat you good in my column from here on in. I'll let you finish out the local show and leave you alone when you go network."

"That *is* pretty white of you at that, Steve."

"See?" Lobeck laughed. "I knew we could talk turkey. I'll kind of nuzzle at you a little now and then once you're network about my friend Whippy, and I'll ask you to give him a good play, but you can rest assured I'll never let my column hurt you. Settled, check? Why don't we drink on it?"

"Sure," Jim nodded, rising and stalking to the bar. "You let me off easy at that." He picked up the ice bucket that Arnie had filled, carried it to Lobeck, opened it, and let three dozen cubes descend over the columnist's head.

"You son of a ..." Lobeck cried.

As he jumped up, Jim shot a rage-driven fist into his stomach and pushed him back to the chair. Striding to the door, he locked it, and walked back. "You're as safe as in your mammy's arms now, you vicious bastard. No one can rush in and protect me. Stand up like the two-fisted journalist you are and throw the next punch."

"You're crazy, you're absolutely out of your head, you crazy jerk," Lobeck called hoarsely. "Weren't you listening to me? I can ruin you! I can write a column and leave you for dead! If you're too damn dumb to play ball with me, I can ..."

"Fine. Let's play some ball," Jim cried and grabbed a fistful of the paling Lobeck's shirt. Bringing him to his feet, Jim fiercely sent another clenched right at his jaw and stepped back, waiting for him to defend himself. When he attempted only to retreat, there was another fist and then another. Dragging him away from the area of the chair, he pushed Lobeck to the closest wall, hearing the crack of shoulder bone against wood, and hurtled himself with all the remaining fury in him toward the man he despised, the man who, like Andrew Creighton, thought that life was a ribboned soiree that imposed responsibilities only on others. His fists, containing all the anguish collected from the years of indecision and uncertainty pummeled at the man called Steve Lobeck. Only distantly did he hear screams for mercy and he was incapable of stopping even when he saw the spurts of blood.

He released himself from the man only after it became dazedly clear that he might commit murder. The bangings at the other side of the door were furious, pleading. He lunged at Lobeck, once more, forcing his fist once more into the man's belly, and shoved him in the direction of the bar. Struggling feverishly to catch his breath, to hear his heart beat in some semblance of controlled order, he contemptuously regarded Lobeck, the blood-splattered face, the suddenly unnerving grimace that lacked at least two front teeth, the stiffened hands that clutched desperately, painfully at his stomach.

The cries from outside and the knocks increased in volume and imperiousness. Finally, aware that nothing in his life would ever be the same again, Jim Creighton clumped to the door, found the key and opened it, and stood back. The raft of Rockland workers, Bucky Stander among them, poured in, and horror enlivened all their faces.

"You're an uninvited guest in my office," Jim told Lobeck. "Get out. Get out now."

Lobeck reeled forward, still embracing himself. "I want an ambulance," he shrieked. "I'm hurt. Somebody get me an ambulance."

"You can still walk," Jim said. "It won't work. There's an elevator to your left. Get on it. If I ever see you again, I'll finish the job."

He ushered everyone out, Bucky included, and then locked the door. Weakly staggering back to the direct center of his office, he heard the telephone ring. It had been ringing endlessly, he suddenly recalled, almost from the time he had dropped the contents of the ice bucket. Still breathing heavily, he trudged to the receiver, peering at the wall clock and observing that he should be getting ready to go down to the *Hot Spot* studio.

"Hello," he said.

"Jim?" Ginny's voice.

"Yes. Jim."

"Jim darling, I've been trying and trying to get you. I need you. I need you at once. He called. Lee called. He's coming over."

"I have a show at ten."

"Don't you understand? Lee's coming here. I've locked the door and all the windows, but he'll be here! This is different from the other time, I know it is. I'm frightened, Jim. I'm scared to run away from here now, I'm scared to move. Jim dearest, please come! Please come!"

"You'll do fine, Ginny," Jim responded. "Your gift of gab and pretty wiggle would get you out of Moscow and into Palm Beach if you shot Khrushchev and in no time at all. See you later, Ginny."

"Jim …"

He replaced the receiver. He helped himself to a stiff shot of the Bell's, straightened his necktie, washed his face, and silently walked past the horde of excited hand-wringers in the corridor to the elevator.

In the studio he pretended that nothing had happened upstairs, greeted both Rufus Neall and Ned Travis, calmly explained that they had nothing to worry about, that the show had been well documented and would be over before they knew it, and did either of them have a cigarette? After a minute or two, the hopeful expectancy of looking up and seeing Evelyn conducting the orchestra from the fish bowl vanished, and he put her out of his thoughts. Here and there he stumbled, repeated himself, stuttered, and felt once or twice that he couldn't make the finish. But the half hour did pass, and by the time he saw Juggy making those calisthenic movements with his fingers, he knew that it at last was over.

Bucky was livid as Jim finished shaking hands with Neall and Travis and thanking them for coming on the show. Yanking him off to a neutral empty corner, Bucky blistered, "I don't know what you were trying to prove upstairs, kicking a critic around, but you're going to pay for it. The law's right outside in the lobby."

"With warrants?"

"You stupid, half-baked country bumpkin! Can't you figure what this is gonna mean? You're tangling with the press! The camera boys from every sheet and syndicate and wire service in New York'll be clicking every part of you all the way to jail! Lobeck yelled assault with intent to kill! You're Jim Creighton, not some stumblebum, and I got my whole life staked on you! What happened, you think you were sacred, that you could hit a newspaperman and he'd forget it? You're in trouble now, kid, and like never before in your dumb luck life!"

The law comprised two plainclothesmen who gave every evidence of wishing they could have locked up Lobeck, instead. "Can I go upstairs and change my clothes before you take me to the chair?" Jim asked.

"Take your time," encouraged the squat man, the one who'd introduced himself as Greenwood. "Thompson and I've been talking outside with the studio guard, Maxie. Maxie was on the force for a hell of a lot of years before they retired him, and he's ace high with us. He says you're ace high, too, and he'll personally vouch for you."

"Thanks. Thanks a lot," Jim said. "I'll be right down."

The telephone in his office was ringing dolefully again as he entered it. Again he heard Ginny's voice.

"You ... let me down ... didn't you?" she whispered. "You said you loved me, and you let me down ..."

"Ginny!" he pressed.

There was a strange, muffled scuffling at the other end of the line, and what seemed to be another voice, a man's voice, breathing harshly, breathing stertorously. And then there was the deafening sound of her receiver being slammed against its cradle.

Jim replaced his phone and raced in terror for the elevators. Emerging onto the street, he ran for the nearest taxi and called out her address. He hurried up her apartment stairs, making three and four steps at a time, and came to her door. It was ajar and he darted in.

She was on the living room couch. She was wearing the same skin-smooth gown she had worn for him after Monica Ender's party. Her wonderful body was lying on the couch, the hem of the gown modestly tucked in about the naked ankles, the self-satisfied smile formed on her marvelously coral lips.

There was blood on her gown, and she was dead.

CHAPTER FIFTEEN

"YOU'RE A LITTLE LATE, aren't you, Creighton?" Lee Gardiner asked pleasantly, materializing from the bedroom, listlessly holding the knife Ginny had described so well. "Shouldn't you have come a bit sooner? You might have saved her. No, I guess not. Maybe not. She knew I would have done it, sooner or later."

"Oh, you bastard," Jim muttered huskily. "You poor, miserable bastard."

"The singular thing about Virginia was that she kept asking for it," Gardiner said, acting judiciously sober as he sat on the edge of her couch. "You involved yourself from the first cloud of perfume, didn't you, so you never recognized that she wanted to be killed. The way other people want to live, but oh, ever so much more discreetly."

"You'll bum for this, Gardiner."

"Yes, of course. Do you think I ever thought I wouldn't?" As Jim advanced, Gardiner lifted the knife. "Don't try to punish me, Creighton," he declared evenly. "I've taken considerably more than most men take, and I don't intend to give in as easily as I gave in to Virginia. You can't understand this, but I had to do it. I loved her and hated her and loved her, on and off and on and off like a cheap hotel's neon sign, from the time we grew up together in Philadelphia." Gardiner waited, then winked. "Did she tell you she was from the South? Or from Canada? Or Europe or Cape Cod? Sure, one of those. But she was from Philly, Creighton. Her name was Virginia Osterwald, and she lived in Germantown next door to me, and she was an ambitious tramp from the time she was eleven." He glanced at her, touched her shoulder, and commended, "Weren't you, Virginia?"

"It had to be this way, Creighton," he went on unhurriedly. "And there aren't any hurt feelings, I'm sure. Virginia wouldn't have really wanted it any other way. What name did she give you—Mrs. Gordon? Mrs. Grant? Mrs. Gray? Husband killed in the war, or shortly thereafter? No dice. Virginia was full of great stories, but she never married. There wasn't time. There was time only to seek out the weak men, to get her teeth into them and destroy them. Like she finally did to me. Like she almost managed to do to you in just about record time."

"Move away," said Jim. "I'm going to call the police."

"Don't try it, Creighton," Gardiner warned. "I have every intention of killing myself. There's no earthly reason why I shouldn't take you along with me for the ride."

Gardiner sat up and appeared pleased with himself. "The reason is easy. We deserve to die when we've had our chances and can't live with dignity. I couldn't and you can't. Why should we clutter up a world that has too few dignified people, as it is? Virginia knew that. She knew that from the time she swiped my typewriter in Germantown when we were just getting out of grade school. She wanted to be all things to all men ... that was her calling, her dedication ... and because that wasn't possible, she killed those weak sisters along the way. You take one more step and I'll slice this down you with no trouble at all!"

Jim leapt forward, wrested the knife from him and chopped the side of his hand against Gardiner's neck. Wholly conscious of what the next few hours would bring, he phoned the police, told them the address and what had happened, and replaced the receiver. Then he fell to a chair, gazed at Ginny, and discovered that he was weeping.

"I saved you, Creighton," said Gardiner. "I, the one who took it and took it all from her. I saved you from becoming me. She fed and drained and dredged and sought out every inch of me that was ready to be knifed. I saved you. Do you honestly think I didn't?"

"No," Jim answered after a moment, staring at the lifeless body of the girl who had told him she loved him. "No, I suppose not."

The story forced every other wire service proclamation off the New York front pages for more than a week. Flanders Bryce Redmond told reporters that he had complete faith in his belief that Jim Creighton, a happily married man, was an unfortunate bystander in this unhappy event, and that nothing could occur to affect his future with *Hot Spot*. But the wildfire gossip ran through the trade that the network sponsor was going to back out, and that Creighton would be replaced the moment the heat began to recede.

Steve Lobeck, who suffered a cracked rib and a half dozen minor damages, instructed his attorney to bring suit against Jim, and advised his readers, "I am not forcing this issue out of any personal anger. When a journalist is unsafe from the Creighton-ilk, who, then, can rightfully call himself safe?" One day later, Lobeck received two numbing shocks. His full column, detailing every juicy fact he had learned about Jim Creighton, was not printed. An hour afterward he was phoned by *The Dispatch*'s publisher, who advised him that he would be paid for the remainder of his contract, but that he no longer was employed. In his usual space, this announcement was run in all editions:

"After careful consideration, we believe that Steve Lobeck's column, *Video, U.S.A.*, no longer serves a useful purpose. Replacing fact and opinion with innuendo and vindictiveness far removed from our concept of responsible criticism, Mr. Lobeck's remarks have become increasingly repugnant to many of our readers and to ourselves. We do not regret his departure."

Harry Creighton spent all the time he could spare with his brother. "Have you seen Fran?" he asked.

"She'll be here this afternoon," Jim replied and noticed that Harry seemed to be waiting for more. "We'll talk, Harry. For the first time in eight years we'll talk to one another. I don't know where it will end up, but I'll tell her everything. I'm going to try to be honest with her and with myself. I owe it to both of us, don't I?"

"And the job? Redmond will want the whole story."

"I can't weasle out of that, either. Bucky has other ideas, and I can't blame him. Bucky wants me to deny everything, to keep ignoring Lobeck, to swear that I never had anything to do with Ginny. To say that I ran down there that night simply because she needed help." Jim lighted a cigarette and closed his eyes. "But I can't do it any more, Harry. I've spent my life avoiding jams … never lying, but never being quite honest, either. You were right when you said a time comes when a man's got to see himself as a man."

The telephone rang. Redmond's secretary said that the boss would be ready to see him in an hour.

"What can I do to help?" Harry asked, as Jim prepared to leave for RBS.

"Not a thing, Harry," he smiled. "This trip's on me. It's about time, isn't it?"